'I want you in every sense of the word, Alexia.'

York continued, 'I want you to play a far greater role in my life than you've been doing. In my life. In my home. In my bed.'

'Permanently? You mean...?' Alexia's eyes desperately searched his. He couldn't be serious. Could he?

'Marry me.' He managed to make it sound more like an order than a request.

'Marry you? I can't. I—'

'Why can't you?' His gaze raked over the tense contours of her face...

Elizabeth Power was born in Bristol where she lives with her husband in a three-hundred-year-old cottage. A keen reader, as a teenager she had already made up her mind to be a novelist, although it wasn't until around thirty that she took up writing seriously. As an animal lover, with a strong leaning towards vegetarianism, her interests include organic vegetable gardening, regular exercise, listening to music, fashion and ministering to the demands of her adopted, generously proportioned cat!

Recent titles by the same author:

JILTED BRIDE

MARRYING THE ENEMY!

BY
ELIZABETH POWER

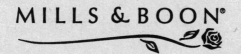

MILLS & BOON®

MILLS & BOON and MILLS & BOON with the Rose Device are registered trademarks of the publisher.

First published in Great Britain 1997
Harlequin Mills & Boon Limited,
Eton House, 18-24 Paradise Road, Richmond, Surrey TW9 1SR

© Elizabeth Power 1997

ISBN 0 263 80108 X

Set in Times Roman 10 on 10½ pt.
01-9705-61760 C1

Printed and bound in Great Britain
by Mackays of Chatham PLC, Chatham

CHAPTER ONE

THE clod of earth made a dull sound on the coffin as the last of the mourners dispersed, leaving Alex standing alone before the open grave.

Page Masterton. Her supposed grandfather. The man who had ruined his own daughter's life and then called on his estranged granddaughter to... To what? Forgive him in his old age?

A shadow, more ominous than the shifting soil, fell across the grave, causing her breath to catch, her insides to tighten with a stomach-churning anticipation. She knew, even before she turned round, that it would be York. York Masterton, whose entrepreneurial ventures she had followed even from the other side of the world, and an insidious tension stole through her as she turned to meet the harsh austerity of his dark, strikingly etched features.

'Would you mind telling me who you are?'

His deep voice was as cold as the raw frost that hadn't melted despite the vain attempts of the bright March sun, and beneath her black three-quarter-coat Alex shivered.

'You mean you don't know me, York? Your only cousin?' There was no affection, only bitter sarcasm in her testing response, because hadn't he been as instrumental as Page all those years ago in hastening Shirley's sad end?

She observed his shocked surprise with a little twist of satisfaction. It wouldn't be like the chief executive of Mastertons, Britain's biggest name in quarrying and civil engineering, to be nonplussed, and he would be chief—totally in control—now that his uncle had died.

'Alexia?' Entirely thrown though he was, he still cut a dominating figure—the long, dark coat he wore over a dark suit, and his sleek black hair filling her with the fanciful, unsettling notion of a raven swooping over its prey. He was, however, merely frowning down at her, those grey-green eyes—which, with that lean, hard-structured face, were so suggestive of his Irish ancestry—disbelieving as he breathed again in a voice that held no trace of the Gaelic accent, *'Alexia?'*

She held her breath, and her gaze wavered for a moment beneath the piercing clarity of his. How could she convince him—or anyone else for that matter—that she was Alexia Masterton when she couldn't even convince herself?

Her chin lifted in an unconsciously rebellious gesture. 'Alex.' Her tone was clipped and concise.

'Alex.' He repeated the name as though giving it careful consideration. 'You used to hate being called that.'

She swallowed. 'Did I?'

He didn't respond, except with that cool, contemplative gaze.

'Well...Alex...' He took a step towards her, the power of his masculinity so overwhelming her that she would have moved back if it had not been for the scrape of the grave diggers' spades behind her. 'This is a surprise, though I must say I would never have recognised you.'

She laughed now, a small, tight sound. Well, no, you wouldn't, would you? she thought drily, but said only, 'I suppose I've matured a bit...'

'A *bit*?' His exclamation held harsh incredulity. 'You've changed beyond all recognition!'

Well, what had she expected him to say? She knew she would have been pushing her luck if she had hoped he would see some resemblance between her and the awkward teenager he'd known for that brief period, but she merely shrugged and glanced away.

Outside the small country church, groups of darkly clad figures still hovered, waiting to pay their respects.

Behind, the Somerset hills rose, sharply white in contrast, glittering under the late frost.

'I was just a kid.' How had he managed with just one look to make her feel exactly what she was—a total intruder?

'A kid who was nicely rounded if not plump.' His remark seemed to give him licence to regard the willowy lines of her body with a thoroughness that was overtly sexual—albeit suspicious—awakening her to the full force of an attraction that only she knew had driven the young Alexia almost crazy with shame. 'A stammering seventeen-year-old with glasses.'

'That was ten years ago.' The sudden tremor in her voice was unmistakable, causing a cruel smile to lift one corner of his mouth. 'I outgrew the puppy-fat with the specs.'

A nerve seemed to quiver in that strong jaw as his gaze flicked inevitably upwards. 'You were also a brunette.'

There was scepticism in every lean inch of him. But he had had to mention it, hadn't he? she thought tensely, feeling his gaze resting with hard contemplation on her hair. She had tried low-lights when it had started greying, then, out of desperation, she'd worn it short and blonde for a while, when the paler strands had become too significant to hide. But by the time she was twenty-five she had given up the battle and started growing it again, so that now it touched her shoulders in a sea of waves beneath the loosely flowing black hood, in her natural colour, soft silver, which with her velvety black brows and blue eyes gave her a uniqueness she had, for some time now, been forced to accept.

'Not everyone's as perfect as you, York,' she uttered, dragging her gaze reluctantly down over his hard, lean physique before sidestepping away from him. At thirty-six—if her calculations were correct—he was the perfect specimen of untrammelled masculinity and didn't even possess one grey strand on that arrogant head!

'Exactly why have you come here?'

'You wrote to me, remember?'

'Did I?'

The doubt in his voice made her back stiffen as she turned, but over her shoulder she threw back disdainfully, 'You know you did.'

'All right, supposing I did? That was over six weeks ago. Pity you couldn't have managed to get here while he was still alive!' His condemnatory tones followed her across the frozen grass. 'But then why bother—when you probably guessed he'd already made you a substantial beneficiary in his will?'

She turned back and cast a quick glance up at him, her eyes guarded, concealing any emotion. She hadn't even considered that the late, wealthy businessman might have left his only grandchild anything...

'Isn't that what you were hoping?' His hard, accusing tone said he believed she *had* considered it—and above everything else.

'No,' she said quietly, the cold that penetrated the thin soles of her low-heeled shoes making her shiver. She'd forgotten how long the winter could linger in England.

'Oh, come on...Alex.' That crease between the thick masculine brows, the way he hesitated over her name told her that, not surprisingly, he still wasn't convinced that she was who she said she was—wasn't absolutely sure. 'Why else would you have flown twelve thousand miles from New Zealand just to arrive right on cue here today? And don't try to convince me it was out of a loving granddaughter's devotion, or you would have come as soon as you'd realised he was ill.'

He was right, but what could she tell him? That she hadn't got his letter? That she'd only recently changed address in Auckland and that his communication had taken five weeks to catch up? Everyone knew there had been virtually no contact and certainly no affection between Page Masterton and his granddaughter in twenty-seven years, and she doubted if this hard, cynical nephew of his would believe an excuse like that.

As for coming here today—a perfect stranger—because that was what she was—what could she say to him? How could she explain her reasons when she wasn't even sure what they were herself? Perhaps she just wanted justice for the unfortunate Shirley and her wretched little offspring, but she had ceased to associate herself with either of them for so long that she wasn't sure any more.

Or perhaps it was because she, Alex Johns, all alone in the world, had once so ached to belong to a family— no, not just any family, *this* family, she thought, with bitter self-recrimination—that she had followed their enterprises through those specially ordered English newspapers with a rapacity that had bordered on the obsessional. She only knew that when she had come home from the studios last week and found lying on the mat that crumpled letter that began, ''My dear Alexia...'' the desire to give in to what remained of those reckless, adolescent yearnings had proved too much.

Her mind clamped tight against the feelings that had ravaged her then. But if York Masterton knew for a moment one of the main reasons why she had been motivated to come...

She shuddered, staring sightlessly at the stone monuments and marble carvings around the little churchyard, guessing at the degree of verbal brutality he could be capable of.

'You didn't give a damn about him.' Those censuring masculine tones flayed her. 'Otherwise you would have been here weeks ago—as soon as you received my letter. Do you think I went to all the trouble of trying to trace you for the fun of it? If it had been left to me I would have—'

He broke off, the lean angles of his face looking drawn—drawn with grief for his uncle, she was astute enough to realise. But there was a bitter detestation in him, too, of her, and quietly she taunted, 'You would

have done what, York? Left me to rot?' Raw bitterness
percolated through her words. 'Like your uncle did with
Shirley?'

She saw anger flare in those grey-green eyes before it
gave way to a question—analysing, diamond-hard.

'Shirley?'

Alex took a breath, steeling herself against his cynical
probing. 'She was only nineteen when she had me, York,
you know that. We were more like sisters. Surely you
can't have forgotten how she didn't like me calling her
anything else? I suppose she didn't like having to admit
I was her daughter.'

'But you've no qualms about admitting it?'

His voice was coldly sarcastic and a wave of colour
washed up over Alex's face. Did he mean because of
Shirley's volatile, fiercely rebellious nature? Or was he
testing her, looking for some inconsistency…? She almost
wanted to turn and run.

'Anyway, it *was* up to you, wasn't it?' she said
pointedly, refusing to let his sarcasm and his obvious
suspicions get to her. 'So why did you—write to me, I
mean? Did Page specifically request you to?'

'No.'

So he had tried to find his late cousin's missing
daughter solely on his own initiative. For some reason
that disturbed Alex far more than if it had been at the
other man's instigation.

'He wouldn't have admitted to it, but I knew he wanted
me to find his only grandchild. As for myself.. ' his
mouth took on a humourless curve as he regarded her
again with that studied insolence '…perhaps I was
curious enough to wonder what Shirley's daughter had
grown up to be. From the teenager I remember I half
expected to find her eking out an existence in one of the
seedier parts of London.'

Alex's hands curled into tight, tense fists. Was that
what he thought had happened to her?

'I hadn't anticipated her running off to New Zealand—let alone changing her name—like someone determined never to be found.'

Perhaps she had been, Alex thought with a sudden, swift dart of anguish that caused her eyes to darken, but, picking up on his words, quickly she said, 'Her? You mean me.'

An eyebrow tilted as he murmured silkily, 'Of course,' but the scepticism was still mirrored in his eyes. Obviously her claim to be his second cousin had thrown him more than she had anticipated. 'It took three months of searching before I'd even picked up a trace.'

But somehow, with the help of that expensive missing persons bureau, he had assumed a link between Alexia Masterton and Auckland television programme researcher Alex Johns and acted upon it.

'Full marks for enterprise, York.' Another little shudder ran through her that was to do with more than just the bitter morning. 'But then you always were resourceful.'

His mouth quirked. 'How do you know? We only met once.'

Was he testing her again? She drew herself up to her full height, which, tall as she was, still left her feeling strangely overshadowed by his dominating stature.

'Twice,' she corrected him. 'The first time for little more than a week. The second a year later—after Shirley died—when you came to ask—no, demand—that I came home.'

The subtle movement of an eyebrow was his only acknowledgement of that sudden little burst of rebellion. 'But you didn't, did you?' he said. 'You ran away instead.' His eyes seemed to dissect her before he smiled superficially. 'Full marks for remembering, Alex. Or are you simply as resourceful as I am?'

She swallowed, looking up at him, a wariness clouding the deep sapphire of her eyes. God! He would be lethal to anyone who imagined they could make a fool of him, she thought, but said only, 'What's that supposed to mean?'

Beneath the expensive coat a broad shoulder lifted in casual dismissal, so that she breathed, 'Are you honestly saying you're actually doubting who I am?'

The lean contours of his face tightened before he sent a glance over his shoulder as doors were thrown closed on the gleaming black saloon cars outside the church.

'You wouldn't be the first to turn up laying claim to being Page's long-lost granddaughter. Since he died we've had reporters lying in wait like a pack of starved wolves, hoping for news of the elusive Alexia, morning, noon and night. Thanks to my cousin's determination to hurt her father—even down to that last act of killing herself— this family's affairs are no longer granted the anonymity they should be—in private matters at any rate!'

'So you think I'm one of them? One of these . . . fallacious claimants?' she uttered, indignant at the callous way he had referred to his cousin's death, though those sharply honed edges of his intellect were stripping her nerves bare. 'Anyway, don't you think my mother told me everything there was to know about you that I didn't know already?' she appended brittly. 'You and Page?'

'Your mother? Shirley?' A cynical smile played around his lips. 'Whatever she told you—for whatever reason— I needn't ask if it was all bad, need I?' he said. 'My cousin had a talent for spreading untruths about her family—her father in particular—that was second to none. She was nothing but a single-minded, mendacious little tramp.'

Alex caught her breath at the smouldering animosity in him. How was he expecting her to react? With hot retaliation and bitter protestations? Perhaps he was thinking that if she were really Shirley's daughter she would.

'That's just your opinion, York,' she responded, with a calmness that surprised even her. 'She was independent, yes—she had to be to bring up a child single-handed. But I never had any reason to doubt that everything she told me was true.'

'No?' he sneered. 'Are you sure we're talking about the same person?'

He was trying to needle her, she realised, but said quietly, 'Obviously not.' And when he looked at her quizzically, as though half expecting her to come clean and admit to being the impostor he suspected her of being, she added quickly, 'Anything she said about either of you, you deserved.'

Too well she knew how Page Masterton had totally governed his daughter's life, preventing her from marrying the man she loved. 'It's not every woman who's lucky enough to have a father who thinks so much of her that he shows it by threatening to call in a debt and bankrupt her fiancé's family if the boy dares to even consider marrying into his. Only she was pregnant, but Page didn't tell him that. He just *arranged* for a convenient job for him abroad.

'And when Shirley rebelled by leaving home—when he couldn't break her into being the adoring daughter he wanted her to be—he tried to get even by attempting to separate her from her own daughter on the only occasion she did come back—and with your help! Perhaps this isn't the time or the place to say it, but Page ruined her life—and you know it.'

His gaze lifted briefly as a rook took off with a distracting cry across the churchyard, and his smile was frozen—like the grass—as he drawled, 'My dear, you really have been misguided.'

'Have I?' Alex's hood slipped back, freeing soft silver waves as she tossed her head indignantly. 'But then you would stand up for him, wouldn't you?' she breathed in a bitterly censorious voice. 'He wanted a son and you filled that role quite adequately, didn't you?'

The firm lines of his mouth twisted in mocking disdain. 'Hardly!'

'No wonder she felt pushed out.'

'Pushed out?' His laugh split the air with a cloud of warm breath. 'My dear young woman, you don't know what you're talking about,' he rasped. 'By the time she'd made her bed I was little more than ten—scarcely old enough to have had any influence on the path of self-destruction she was already headed down and you know it. And you're right—' anger tightened the muscles of his chest beneath the pristine shirt '—this isn't the time or the place.'

She would have liked to tell him that she knew exactly what she was talking about, because, above all else, in the beginning, before the rot had set in—before circumstances had driven her into the reckless lifestyle that had killed her—Shirley had been her closest friend.

His last remark, though, had effectively silenced her—which was just as well, she realised, because two elderly women were approaching, one of them stopping a polite distance away as the taller of them singled York out.

'York, I'm going back to the house in Brigette's car so you'll not need to be worrying about me. The service was beautiful, wasn't it?' she added approvingly, before her interest settled on the slim young woman at his side.

His smile for the older woman was warm, none of his animosity towards Alex allowed to show through the exterior charm, so that only she sensed the scorn behind it when he suddenly said, 'Mother, would you believe that this confident, silver-haired creature is the long-lost Alexia?' And then he added startlingly to Alex, 'You remember my mother?'

Studying the grey-haired lady in the elegant dark wool suit, Alex felt all her composure deserting her. Was she supposed to? Because York Masterton clearly thought she should. But she couldn't even remember Shirley's ever saying she'd met his mother. Hadn't both his parents moved to Ireland, which was where his paternal grandfather had come from? And hadn't York stayed in

England to finish his schooling before going into the family business because he'd got on better with Page—his step-uncle—than he had with his own father?

'You mean . . . this is Page's granddaughter?'

As the woman whispered her surprised disbelief Alex could feel York's hard scrutiny. Unconsciously, her nails dug into her palms. What was he expecting her to say? That she remembered his mother vividly? And what was he going to do? Expose her as a fraud? Pick her up bodily and cart her off to the nearest police station if she said she didn't?

Surprisingly, the thought of his handling her made her veins pulse with something more unwelcome than just the revulsion and resentment she knew she should only have room for, and, striving for something intelligible to say that wouldn't further increase his suspicions about her, she couldn't have been more relieved when his mother chipped in.

'It's gratifying to see you here, dear. Let us hope that now we can begin to put the past behind us. I'm Celia, if you weren't already aware,' she elucidated, her kind, friendly manner causing a pang of guilt in Alex because she wasn't exactly here to make peace with the family as Celia thought.

'But really, York,' the woman went on, amiably reprimanding her son, 'your memory doesn't usually let you down. You must be overworking, darling, or keeping your mind on too many other things, otherwise you'd have remembered me saying only recently that I'd never had the chance to meet Shirley's daughter.'

Well, thank heaven for that! Breathing a sigh of relief, Alex smilingly made some appropriate response, and from under her lashes sent a cursory glance towards the tall man beside her.

He was looking smug, as though he'd enjoyed her moment of discomfort, even if it had backfired on him before he'd been able to expose her to what she realised

now was his sheer, machiavellian cunning. Then the
second woman had moved across to him, smiling her
appreciation for what she clearly saw as a very per-
sonable man as she expressed a few fond remarks about
his uncle and stepped away.

'I hope I'll see you back at the house and that we'll
have some time to get to know each other, Alexia, before
I leave for Dublin,' Celia said with warm sincerity.

'Yes.' It wasn't a very positive response from Alex.
She didn't want to go anywhere where York was likely
to be—and that included the house—although she wasn't
sure how she could avoid it if she was to find what she
had come for. But, grateful for a flicker of warmth from
one member of the Masterton family, she added,
'Thanks. I hope so too.'

York's expression was unfathomable, so that she
couldn't tell what he was thinking as he watched the two
older women walking away. But, on finding herself disconcertingly alone with him again, Alex's chin came up
and, despite her pumping heart, she breathed, 'You can't
intimidate me, York.'

'Can't I?' The firm, thrusting lines of his jaw
harshened as he gave her his full attention again. 'Maybe
not,' he conceded. 'But if you think you can just walk
in here and stake a claim on my uncle's generosity
without my doing anything to stop you, you've got
another think coming!'

His determination unnerved her. Nevertheless, in spite
of it she managed to smile.

'That should be interesting.' Whatever Page Masterton
had left his granddaughter, *she* wasn't likely to be making
any claim to it. Even so, she couldn't help taunting, 'And
I thought you were rich enough, York.' From the things
she'd read about him it seemed he'd made millionaire
status ten times over! 'What ever could he have left me
that could possibly make any difference to you?'

The grass crunched under his highly polished black
shoes as he followed her down onto the path towards

the church. 'We're going to require concrete evidence from you as to exactly who you are before we even begin to think about discussing *that*.'

Alex drew in a breath, colour rising in her cheeks. 'I don't have to prove anything to you!'

His eyes were astute, missing nothing. 'Spare me the indignation, lady,' he advised. 'It's going to take more than that to convince me... Alex. And my uncle's solicitors are going to need more than just a sultry smile and that sexy New Zealand accent before they agree to grant you the half-share of the house.'

'Half the house? Is that what he left...?' Me, she had been going to finish with, but stopped herself short. She had no right to it. Nor did she want it—any of the Masterton money.

'Over my dead body,' he whispered, the venom in him causing a slick of fear to infiltrate her blood.

Hadn't she learned from everything she had read about him—from his hard-nosed business acumen down to the hidden forces of his personality—how tough he was? Hadn't Shirley warned her? Why, then, had she imagined she could come here like this?

'If I'd been Page I would have disinherited you entirely.'

'But he didn't.' Unexpectedly, something stirred in Alex—something she banked down before it could manifest itself into anything more concrete as she uttered, 'And you resent that like hell, don't you?'

The hard glitter in his eyes confirmed it, but it was resentment born solely out of his contempt for Shirley and whoever he thought *she* was, she was surprised to find herself acknowledging, rather than any sort of greed on his part.

'Wouldn't *you*,' he returned, 'if you'd seen a man virtually destroy himself because of the total disregard by his only daughter, and when her avaricious, alleged little offspring turns up to get her hands on the only thing Shirley didn't already bleed him of—his money?'

She doubted if Page Masterton had ever cared enough
about his daughter to suffer any sort of emotional trauma
over her desertion, but all she said was, '"Alleged",
York?' From beneath her lashes she slanted him a glance
that was both challenging and watchful. 'Are you still
insinuating I'm not who I say I am?'

They had come to a standstill on the path. Beneath
the bare trees York's face was criss-crossed by shadows.

'Are you?' he demanded, his eyes narrowing with cold
calculation.

Alex's breathing stilled beneath the stylish cut of her
coat. How Shirley's intimidated little daughter would
have savoured seeing him in such a state of ambiv-
alence—so undecided—ten years ago!

She laughed, the sound easy on the cold, clear air.
'You really don't know, do you? And that's what's really
bugging you, isn't it, York? The fact that you aren't really
sure. Just for once you aren't completely in control and
you can't stand it, can you...cousin dear? Well, you'll
just have to accept my word for it, won't you?' she finished, with bitter irony twisting her mouth.

His smile was slick, without warmth, cold as the day.
'Accept the word of anyone who calls herself Shirley's
daughter? Hah! That's laughable in itself! But whatever
you are—freeloading little tramp or total charlatan—I'm
warning you now, I'm a very dangerous man to cross.
Make one false move—just one mistake—and I'll...'

'You'll do what?' she retaliated, undeterred by his
threatening tone. 'Clap me in irons?'

His eyes mocked her response, her whole defiant
stance. 'Is that how you like to play? Bound and begging
for mercy? Not quite the little innocent who came to my
bedroom expecting chaste kisses.'

A heated flush stole into the translucent sheen of her
cheeks. Oh, stupid, stupid fool! What was she letting
herself get into? Why had she imagined she could come
here without inviting a whole heap of trouble? Yet—
from another life, it seemed—reluctantly she was aware

of how his body would feel beneath her hands, of the hard, burning arousal of his kisses. Because Alexia had known. But that Alexia was dead. And all *she* had to do was play the part until her purpose here was accomplished...

'Unlike you,' she said softly, refusing to be swayed by the power of his sexuality, 'I've always been rather particular with whom I play.'

He chuckled at that. Perhaps he didn't mind being reminded that he had once been photographed with an actress who'd later become mixed up in a pretty hair-raising scandal. 'An unfortunate liaison,' he said dismissively.

'Very,' she said pointedly, although she knew that his integrity had emerged unscathed.

'Nevertheless, until I'm satisfied as to exactly who you are, you'll be coming back to Moorlands with me where I can keep an eye on you for however long it takes.'

For however long what took? Proving her false identity? Was that what he was hoping for?

'I'm doing no such thing! I've got a very adequate hotel room in town, thanks!' she snapped, deciding that staying under the same roof with this man could lead her into nothing but trouble. 'Naturally I'll want to—' she started, but he cut in, his expression inexorable, his mouth grim.

'You'll do exactly as I say.'

She wanted to argue against it, but that overriding determination in him—that tyrannical streak that she knew very well was characteristic of the Masterton men—was too strong. It was the reason why Shirley had left home, why she had struggled for an existence on her own with only her child after Page had prevented her marriage, why she'd been dragged down into the unfortunate lifestyle that had led to her overdose. Accidental, the coroner had said, brought about by a lethal blend of booze and barbiturates.

Something speared through Alex—something cutting and deep. Oh, to find some skeleton in the impeccable Masterton cupboard! Particularly in the high and mighty, unimpeachable York's!

But refusing to do as he said, insisting on staying at the hotel, wouldn't help her in trying to convince him that she was his cousin, nor to find those letters which, suddenly, had become the most important things in her life. And so, feigning sweetness, with a totally false smile, she uttered, 'As you put it so hospitably, how can I refuse?'

CHAPTER TWO

MOORLANDS stood in its own grounds on the fringes of a small Somerset resort, a beautifully grey-gabled, Cotswold-style house with fields rising to woodland on one side and the town stretching away to the sea on the other.

As they came up the long drive in York's powerful saloon Alex was relieved that the journey from the church had been a short one, so that she hadn't had to engage in much conversation with him.

'The beech hedge was planted courtesy of Edmundo, our long-standing gardener,' he commented about the copper-leafed boundary fence hung with cobwebs of frost on their right. 'But then you wouldn't remember him, would you?' he breathed derisively, bringing the car around a triangular grassy island with an old and gnarled maple tree at its centre, testing her again—as he would continue to test her, she realised, every step of the way.

'As a matter of fact I do,' she shot back. 'Portuguese, isn't he?' And the only person at Moorlands whom Shirley had spoken of with any affection, she remembered. 'Didn't he come to work here the year my mother was born?'

York slanted her a look that said it would take more than that to impress him. 'Very good,' he drawled. And then he added, 'How old is his son?'

'What?'

He had brought the car between two ivy-covered walls onto the deserted, cobbled forecourt, the look he gave her hard and inquisitorial when she didn't immediately respond.

'He didn't have a son—just two daughters,' she assured him after a long moment's deliberation, colour swamping her cheeks as she went on heatedly, 'If you think I'm going to spend my time here indulging in some sort of question-and-answer game with you, you're very much mistaken, York Masterton! Either you accept me for who I am or you throw me out and let me go back to the hotel, which I'd be more than happy to do!'

He smiled knowingly. 'I'll bet you would!' he said, cutting the engine of the BMW and turning towards her with his eyes anything but friendly. 'Why didn't you come here straight away instead of turning up at the funeral like some fugitive if you've got nothing to hide? Or would that have been too complicated? Did you imagine I'd be at more of a disadvantage meeting you in the churchyard like that, too unsettled by the occasion to think about much else, rather than if you'd faced me here, on my home territory?'

She hadn't reckoned on his being quite so resolute in not believing her. But she had all the papers, so why was he managing to make her feel so unnerved?

'This isn't your home,' was all she could think of to say at that moment. From what she had read in the papers, she'd thought that these days he lived in a luxury apartment in London.

'It is now.' Disconcertingly, his arm came across the back of her seat, and she almost hated herself for the small tingle that ran through her as he leaned across and murmured in a voice of mocking sensuality, 'Mine and yours.' She had to make a conscious effort to desist from inhaling the subtle, tangy spice of his aftershave. 'That should make a very... interesting partnership.'

'A partnership—with you?' she choked, despising her body's totally unwelcome awareness of him. 'I'd rather go into business with a gorilla!'

He laughed without humour, that strong, masculine jaw hardening. 'You've certainly come with some pretty well-conceived opinions about me, haven't you...

cousin?' His tone derided the title. 'Well, for your information, they're all true. But who said anything about business?'

Alex felt her throat working nervously. Whoever he thought she was—his estranged cousin out for all she could get, or a total impostor—he had no qualms about using that powerful masculinity to try and scare her off. Well, he wasn't going to succeed!

Ignoring his innuendo, she uttered nonetheless unsteadily, 'I told you—I didn't come here for the money.'

'Then what for—*if* you're who you say you are?' he demanded, allowing her to breathe again when he moved back, absently taking his keys out of the ignition. 'And you haven't answered my other question. Why were you stalking round the graveyard instead of coming here to see me first?'

Alex bit her tongue to stop herself retorting that she hadn't been 'stalking', as he had put it, advising herself that it would be in her best interests not to antagonise him deliberately.

'I thought you'd answered that yourself. Why, I'm positively terrified of you, aren't I, York?' she couldn't, however, resist tossing back sarcastically with a pale, beautifully manicured hand against her chest. 'The truth is, I didn't get into Heathrow until breakfast-time yesterday morning. It was a twenty-four-hour flight and I'm lucky if I slept for two. Consequently all I was fit for was to book into the nearest hotel and fall into bed, and I didn't wake up until nine o'clock yesterday evening. I only found out then, when I picked up a paper someone had left in the lounge, that Page had died. How do you think I felt, finding out that his funeral was today?'

'Immensely relieved, I would have thought.' His own sarcasm was unrelenting.

'You don't have the slightest sympathy for how I might feel, do you?' she breathed, her teeth clenched as she struggled to control her temper. At least that was one advantage she had over the fiery-natured adolescent he had known. She was more in control.

He would never have a good word to say about Shirley—or anyone connected with her. She should have expected it. 'My mother was born here—even if I wasn't—even if she was regarded as being outside the socially accepted circle for having me. And whatever Page did to her—he *was* my grandfather. You're not the only one who's been blessed with the ability to feel!'

He waited patiently while she finished. She wasn't going to add that she had strong doubts about the last point—doubts about whether he could feel at all—which only increased as he drawled cynically, 'Congratulations on the performance. Do you expect me to believe that you didn't wait until Page was safely out of the way before you risked coming here? Were you hoping I'd be less of a problem to manipulate? Because, if you were, you're in for a pretty rude awakening, Alex Johns—or whatever your real name might be. So what is it if, as you say—' his chin jerked roughly upwards '—it isn't the money?'

Those grey-green eyes were penetrating, causing Alex's tongue to stray across her top lip. Fortunately, though, another car was coming up the drive, drawing York's attention mercifully away from her. What would he have said if she'd told him? she wondered as she opened her door and stepped out into the cold, glittering day.

Half of Moorlands. A generous allowance and a few shares in the business.

As the solicitor and his clerk left, Alex stood numbly by the long leaded window, her arms folded, watching the dark saloon drive away.

'How does it feel—getting things the easy way?'

Alex swung round, her gaze skittering across the plush, classically furnished lounge.

Jacketless, York was standing in the doorway, his hands on his hips, his long, powerful legs astride beneath the tailored trousers. Not many people had come back to the house, but those who had had gone. All except Celia, who was upstairs somewhere getting changed.

'If you need to ask any more questions, why don't you have it out with your solicitor?' she recommended, with a toss of her head towards the window. 'He seemed perfectly satisfied that he was dealing with the right woman.' She felt her throat contract as he came into the room, an animal of such impressionable strength and forcefulness that inevitably her pulses started to quicken.

'I'm not surprised—when you had him eating out of your hand from the word go.'

'That's hardly true,' she reminded him. In fact the solicitor had been a very pleasant but astute middle-aged man. 'And I thought you said he couldn't be charmed by my winning smile.'

His gaze flicked cursorily over her slender figure beneath the pearl-grey silk blouse and straight navy skirt— all that she had been able to find that morning amongst her possessions suitable for wearing to a funeral.

'Maybe I was wrong.' His gaze lifted to assess the creamy smoothness of her complexion, the darkly fringed sapphire of almond-shaped eyes, the wide, sensual mouth, all framed by the intriguing silver of her hair— and in a voice that was dangerously soft he said, 'Is any man immune?'

The tightening in Alex's throat became almost painful and she took an involuntary step back, only to feel the soft cushions of the window-seat against her leg.

'You've got all the charm of a beautiful woman plus a cool, level-headed intelligence. That's a dangerous combination. The Alexia I knew was guileless, passionate, impulsive...'

'She was a child!'

Light played across the rich ebony of that arrogant, tilted head.

' "She"?' he repeated in a voice like soft, suffocating silk.

'So now you've got me doing it!' Impatience coloured her voice. 'What do you think I did with her? Killed her off and stole her identity?' she argued, barely able to keep her mind on what she was saying. He was so dangerously attractive, had such a fascinating lure for the opposite sex that she might have melted under the blaze of that powerful magnetism if she hadn't been so aware of how insensitive he was. 'You saw all my papers!'

'Yes.'

And he had had little choice but to accept them, as the solicitor had—to accept them as authentic, she thought, with a small twist of satisfaction. 'So why are you still insinuating I'm not telling the truth?'

'Why indeed?' He moved a disconcerting step closer, that aura of potent male energy about him as unsettling as his uncomfortable nearness. 'Perhaps it's because under that oh, so cool-as-a-cucumber façade you're remarkably edgy. Unless, of course, by some stretch of the imagination you're telling the truth and it's something much more basic than the need for circumspection that's making you so uneasy in my presence.' Cold mockery gave an upward curl to his mouth. 'Still find me sexy, Alex?'

Despite the bitter frost that seemed to have got through to her bones, even though the house was centrally heated, Alex felt herself grow sticky beneath her blouse.

'Is your conceit innate? Or has it been specially cultivated?' she challenged stiffly, hiding the nervousness that her voice could so easily have revealed.

He laughed. 'All right, if that's the way you want it,' he said. 'I suppose if I'd been Alexia I'd probably have wanted to conceal the more intimate details too.'

Alex swallowed. She knew what he was talking about. She just didn't want to think about it, and for a moment she longed to blurt out what he wanted her to say—that she wasn't Alexia Masterton, she was someone else entirely. But that would have been self-defeating as well as stupid, and, striving for that outward calm he had mentioned, she murmured wearily, 'Have you quite finished?'

A muscle twitched in his jaw and she thought for a moment that he was going to slap her down—metaphorically at any rate—for that little display of audacity. But all he did was stoop to pick up a tissue—hers, she realised—that was lying on the carpet, and, handing it to her, he said, 'You can freshen up upstairs and then we'll drive down into town so that you can pick up your luggage. Then I'll take you round and show you what I'm going to do all in my power to stop you getting your hands on. That's, of course, if you aren't still too jet-lagged.'

So he'd noticed that weariness in her. As he'd notice everything, she couldn't help deciding with a little shudder.

Refusing to be baited into any more arguments with him, though, all she said was, 'No.' And, when he didn't give her any indication of where she was to go, uttered pointedly, 'Could you at least show me where it is—the bathroom, I mean?'

An emotion—impossible to read—flitted across his face. 'You're supposed to have been here before. I would have thought in the circumstances you would have been able to tell me.'

'Very funny,' she returned. 'That was ten years ago. People change their homes. Knock down walls. Build extensions... And anyway, my room had an *en suite*.'

She could see the question in those shrewd, perceptive eyes: was she guessing, or had she simply been informed?

'In that case...' With a gesture of exaggerated politeness he indicated for her to precede him out of the room, guided her across the sunny, tastefully furnished hall and up the curving staircase to the floor above.

'This will be your room.' He threw open one of the doors off the long landing. Sunlight streamed in from the leaded casement windows, spilling across the cream and floral duvet on the double bed.

This room overlooked the back of the house. Outside, the manicured gardens and the sweeping fields rising to the woods still glittered under a silver veil. A picture-book landscape. Lifeless, Alex decided, until she spotted a wisp of smoke drifting upwards from the chimney of a farm building in the distance.

'The bathroom,' she guessed, moving towards a door.

'Wrong.' His voice came, deep and relentlessly testing, from behind her. 'My room. It might seem a little too cosy to you, but at least this way I can keep account of exactly what you're doing.'

Alex's feet pivoted on the pale, patently expensive carpet. 'Is that how you get your kicks?' she breathed accusingly. 'Listening to what your guests get up to?'

York's mouth pulled down at the corners. 'Not usually. But then we haven't exactly established whether you're a guest or not, have we?'

'Haven't we?' she retorted, his suspicions beginning to test her reserves. And, though she hadn't intended using it in any way as a defence, she couldn't help adding, 'I believe I'm co-owner, which surely gives me rights to come and go as I please, or even to bring friends back here if I so think fit?'

She had no intention of doing anything of the sort—she had said it only to show him that she couldn't easily be cowed by his infernal arrogance—because although she got on well with people she was very much a loner. As for men, she had never met anyone who could break down her reserves enough to make her want to sleep with him. Only once. But she wasn't even going to think about that.

'You do and I'll throw you both out,' he rasped, interpreting her remark exactly as he wanted to. 'No part of this house becomes yours until the necessary documentation's drawn up to say that it does.'

'So you'll use strong-arm tactics? Like you did before. Sheer brute strength just so long as you could exercise Page's every last whim in trying to separate Shirley from the one thing she cared about most—her daughter!'

His face appeared to turn savage beneath the raven sleekness of his hair. 'Shirley didn't care about anyone but herself—so don't lay it on that thick, dear child. And never—*never*—breathe a denigrating word to me about my uncle in this house again. And if I'm not too mistaken—' his voice was more controlled and, like his expression, suddenly coolly derisive '—I don't think it would have taken very much persuasion on my part to induce her hot little *daughter* to stay.'

'God! You're conceited!'

'Am I? Perhaps we ought to put it to the test.'

'Don't you dare!'

She didn't know what happened next, only that he had caught the hands that flew up instinctively to fend him off, securing them behind her back, and primitive sensations rushed through her as she found herself locked against his hard body.

'Let me go!' She could barely drag the words past her lips, panic rising in her as he laughed harshly.

'Why? Because it's there now—that attraction, isn't it...cousin dear?' His words mocked, cruelly, relentlessly. 'Is that why you're putting on such a marvellous act of being affronted? Or is it the thought of sex between cousins? That never worried you before. But if Shirley didn't make it clear enough—we're only connected by marriage. Page and my father were only stepbrothers, so if the thought of any blood ties between us bothers you you can stop worrying about that right now.'

'I'm not worried!' she tossed up at him unthinkingly, her face defiant, though the startling reality of his hard strength was making her senses swim.

'In that case—' his mouth took on a sensual curve '—I don't believe I exactly welcomed you the way a cousin should.'

She couldn't have prevented what happened next if she had wanted to—the way his mouth suddenly covered hers, both gentle and yet shockingly erotic, those hands splayed across her back, holding her loosely but ready to turn hard and show their determined power if she dared to resist.

She sensed enough about that to stand still and take it, her mind struggling to reject the sickening excitement that was suddenly rising in her blood, a raw stirring of primitive needs she hadn't anticipated or been prepared for, every cell tensing with her body's acknowledgement of his hard power and his musky male scent beneath the subtle aftershave as his mouth played with leisurely insolence over hers.

His eyes were hooded, veiled by the thick sable of his lashes when he eventually lifted his head.

'No response? And yet no resistance either.'

'What did you imagine?' The hard rise and fall of her breasts was the only indication of her shattered self-composure. 'That if I was who I said I was there would be?'

He started to say something, but Celia's voice in the corridor, exclaiming, 'Oh, there you are!' pulled them apart.

The woman came in, commenting to Alex, 'I trust York's doing everything possible to make you comfortable.'

'Everything,' she heard him drawl meaningfully, when she was still too shaken by his kiss to answer, and she was relieved when his mother, promising to see her downstairs, asked if she could have a word with York about her travel arrangements, which left Alex mercifully alone.

She didn't have to take this! she thought, wiping the back of her hand across her mouth. It smelt of his aftershave lotion and her lips were still tingling from his calculated humiliation. She could go home. Forget about why she had come. It was a long shot, anyway, that she would find those letters. She could go now. Pick up her case and get the train straight back to London. But that would be letting York Masterton get the better of her. And for Shirley's sake—for her own sake—she wasn't going to allow him to do that.

He was dangerously attractive, a threat to any healthy woman's equilibrium, but she just had to make sure that she didn't fall into the trap of succumbing to any tricks he might try and use to get her to weaken before that devastating and shockingly confident sexuality. If she did, she'd be courting trouble, she assured herself chasteningly, reminding herself of how York and his uncle had both played their part in driving Shirley away.

Well, *she* wasn't going to let a Masterton man drive *her* away until she was good and ready! she resolved, with such vehemence that she scarcely noticed the jaded practicality of the *en suite* bathroom she finally found, or the lack of any really homely touches in this late millionaire's home.

The red stone of the quarry gaped like an ugly mouth on the undulating Somerset landscape.

'When my step-grandfather—Page's father—started the company this was where it grew from,' York stated, bringing the car to a standstill outside one of the Portakabins where all the site's immediate adminis- tration was obviously carried out. 'Just a small, family- run business he'd mortgaged to the hilt, supplying raw material to equally small local builders wherever he could.'

'And from this he went into construction.' Small office units at first, Alex remembered Shirley telling her, and, in Page's time, larger, industrial sites, but only York had given the company the real hard-nosed drive and mo- tivation that had made Mastertons the first name in multimillion-pound developments: sports complexes, inner city expansion, whole housing estates—the best in architectural design. She had found all that out herself.

'Quite a success story,' she couldn't help saying appreciatively, with a little shiver of resentment as she pushed
back a thick silver wave behind her ear.

York made a cynical sound down his nostrils. 'And
one that isn't going to end with Little Red Riding Hood
getting a bite-sized chunk of the apple,' he promised,
with sudden, soft vehemence.

She grimaced, glancing down at the redundant hood
falling softly across her shoulder. 'I thought that was
Snow White—who ate the apple,' she enlarged, with a
tartness nonetheless, as if she had just bitten into some
acrid fruit. 'And my hood's black. I'm afraid this little
heroine isn't afraid of the big, bad wolf. You'd still despise me, wouldn't you, York, even if you were sure
about me—for refusing to knuckle under to your demands and come back here like the dutiful granddaughter after Shirley died? For not bowing down to
you and Page like you both expected me to?'

He didn't answer, and, getting out, said only, 'Wait
here,' his expression as cold as the icy draught through
the car that persuaded him to shrug into his thick dark
coat before throwing the door closed after him.

Tight-lipped, Alex watched him, her gaze reluctantly
following his hard, arrogant physique as he mounted the
steps to the Portakabin and disappeared inside.

Way down in the quarry she could hear the continual
drone of heavy equipment, male voices shouting, could
see the red dust cloud as the machinery ate into the hard
rock.

After a while, restless from sitting doing nothing, she
stepped out of the car, pulling up her hood and stuffing
her hands deep into her pockets to protect them from
the freezing air.

She was attracting a lot of looks from men coming in
and out of another Portakabin, she realised after a few
moments of pacing up and down, although she was used
to being the object of men's interest. It was fascination,
she had convinced herself over the years, because of the

uniqueness of her colouring, but in this instance she knew that a lot of the attention was generated by her having been seen arriving with York.

'Hey, that's nice, isn't it?'

'Um, very tasty.'

A soft wolf-whistle followed the rather sexist remarks she knew she had been intended to hear.

'Cut it out, lads.' It was an older man's voice this time. A surreptitious glance from under her lashes showed that the 'lads' to whom he had spoken were barely out of their teens. 'We don't allow that sort of thing on site, and if we did we'd be a bit more particular about who we whistled at. Do you know who that is?' A moment's silence. 'That's Alexia Masterton. The old man's granddaughter.'

'Yikes!'

As surprised as the embarrassed-sounding youth, Alex caught her breath, and over the other sounds rising up into the Somerset hills heard the first youth utter, 'You're kidding! I thought she was dead.'

That carelessly uttered statement sent a cold emotion shivering through Alex.

She must have been mad to come here, she thought, her feet carrying her swiftly over the dusty ground back towards the car. Alexia Masterton had been dead *and* buried and she'd been a fool to resurrect her. But news certainly travelled fast! How could anyone have known?

'Miss Masterton?' She was so lost in thought that the man had to call the name again before she realised that someone was speaking to her. And as she turned he added, 'Would you like a coffee while you're waiting?'

'N-no...thanks.' She offered him a rather wan smile, still regretting what she couldn't help deciding was a total lack of common sense on her part in coming here at all.

'Come on. He could be some time,' the man informed her, with a jerk of his chin towards the cabin where York had gone. He was fiftyish, with smiling, weather-worn features, and as she mentally replaced his thick donkey jacket with the suit in which she now vaguely remembered seeing him that morning it dawned on Alex that he must have overheard someone speak her name outside the church. 'The lads won't eat you. They might look vicious, but one smile from a pretty girl and they'd probably both run a mile.'

A harmony of guffaws rang out from what were now two very red-faced young men. They had been drinking out of tin mugs, but from somewhere had managed to produce a ceramic one for Alex.

The coffee was hot and tasted good, and she was glad the man, who introduced himself as Ron, had talked her into it.

'I hope you're going to be a regular visitor here. This place could do with brightening up a bit.' The man winked at the two youths, whose boldness had disintegrated and who were both totally dumbstruck now that Alex had moved into their sphere, but a small pang of guilt assailed her. She was misleading them—all of them—she thought. Ron was basically a nice man, and how could she explain that she had no intention of staying any longer than she could help, that really she had no right—no right at all—even being here?

'Your grandfather always found time to look in to see how things were doing—when he was able to get about, that was. But then when Mr York—I mean Mr Masterton—took things over—and it's been quite a time now—he never let things slide. He's always kept up the family tradition in keeping himself aware of what's going on here, big as he's become. Even though quarrying—and this quarry in particular—is just a small part of what he's involved with nowadays, he hasn't forgotten those who've been loyal to him and his uncle—and even *his* father before him. He still likes to keep himself involved with any problems or difficulties the men might be facing down here.'

Which was one thing to be said for him, if nothing else! Alex conceded rather begrudgingly.

'My...grandfather...' She felt awkward even using that title to describe Page Masterton. 'He was ill for a long time?' She hadn't got round to asking York just how long it had been.

'Well...' Ron pursed his lips, considering. 'Probably about two or three months.'

She frowned, warming her hands around the hot mug, watching the steam rise, warm and aromatic on the air. 'But I thought you said...'

'Oh, because I said about him getting about?' Ron grimaced. 'Sorry to confuse you. No, I meant because of his wheelchair.'

'His wheelchair?' Alex's frown deepened. She felt utterly flummoxed. 'Oh—oh, of course,' she said. How could she let these people—people who surprisingly but clearly had loved and respected Page Masterton—know that she, apparent claimant to much of his estate, didn't know that he'd been disabled, a cripple? She felt a dryness in her throat that didn't ease even when she swallowed. There was too much she didn't know. Too much, she was gradually realising, that she hadn't taken enough trouble to find out.

'Didn't you find him even a little bit difficult at times?' She smiled, hoping she'd sounded blithe.

'Not at all.' Ron's tone denied any suggestion of it. 'He was the best employer any man could hope to work for. With some...' his shoulders lifted, his mouth pulling down derogatorily into even deeper lines '...wealth goes to their heads and they won't talk to the likes of us. 'Course we always knew he was in charge. There wasn't any questioning his authority. But he was a decent bloke. And I'm pleased to say Mr York—er—Masterton—is carrying on in the same way, although he's got double the energy and the authority. 'Course, he's younger. But it's a good thing with this lot if you ask me.'

Alex sipped the steaming coffee, her smile ruminative as she followed Ron's gesture towards the two bashful-looking youths. It wasn't the picture Shirley had painted of her father—or even of York.

'So how long has it been exactly since Mr Mast—I mean Mr York,' she corrected herself, 'took over the running of things?' Obviously it was a name used privately between the men, she realised, to distinguish between uncle and nephew. She had to find out, acquaint herself with facts she hadn't gleaned simply from Shirley and the newspapers.

'Why don't you ask him yourself?'

Hearing the deep, familiar voice, she whirled around, wincing as hot coffee slopped over her hand.

'That was rather careless.'

Of course he'd noticed, and before she had realised it he was pressing a clean white handkerchief into her hand. It was slightly warm from his body heat and she knew that it would smell of his own personal scent. The scent that had lingered on her skin after he had kissed her...

'Th-thanks,' she stammered, feeling awkward, wishing he hadn't, unable to look at him as he addressed the others.

'Gary, Jason, I don't pay you to stand around all day drinking coffee with the first nubile female that breezes in here.' Like magic, his unquestionable authority had the two teenagers scuttling back to work. 'Thanks for keeping her out of mischief, Ron.' His tone held deep respect for the older man.

When they were back in the car, however, his coat discarded on the back seat, he said scathingly, 'Asking a lot of questions, weren't you?' Suspicion burned in his eyes as he pulled away with more than a fair amount of aggression, the spinning wheels kicking up dust.

'Why shouldn't I ask questions about my family if I want to?' Alex challenged indignantly.

He cast a sidelong glance across the car. '*Your* family?' he sneered. 'I don't think there's any way that I can be fooled into imagining that you have any right here.' And before she could respond he said harshly, 'And did you have to aim your questions at my employees?'

Perhaps I shouldn't have, she thought, studying the nails of one hand which was resting in her lap. They were filed to their usual moderate length, enhanced only by a clear, protective lacquer. Edgily, though, she said, 'Well, I knew the sort of response I'd have got if I'd asked you.'

He didn't look at her as the car climbed the long road out of the quarry.

'That doesn't give you any right to go fraternising with them,' he said. 'Sharing their coffee-breaks, laughing and joking with them as if you were on their level. Familiarising yourself with my workforce, Alex, is, from now on, strictly taboo.'

Alex's nostrils flared as she watched him stop at a junction. The lush Somerset valley dropped away below them, stretching for miles, green touched with silver, from the sparkling lower fields to the thick white caps over the surrounding hills.

'You hypocrite,' she murmured under her breath.

'Hypocrite?' Now, as he pulled away, he sent a questioning glance in her direction.

'Ron said what a decent guy you were. That your position hasn't made you put yourself above them—probably because of the act you put on in trying to convince them it hasn't,' she couldn't refrain from adding, although, strangely, she didn't really believe that. Instinctively she knew that York Masterton wouldn't ever try to be anything but the man he was. 'Now you're implying I shouldn't stoop even to talking to them.'

'Corrupting is the word I'd use,' he delivered with smooth precision. 'And I was thinking more of them—not you.'

'Thanks,' she breathed, and stared belligerently at the road. Well, what could she expect from him? she thought. He didn't trust her. And, even if he did eventually accept her as his long-lost cousin, because of his low opinion of Shirley and the gold-digger he obviously thought she, Alex, was he'd still continue to flay her verbally at the least opportunity.

'I never knew Page was in a wheelchair,' she said tentatively.

'No? Didn't you read it somewhere?' he muttered with scathing emphasis.

Alex swallowed, trying not to be put off. 'No.'

'He was in it long enough,' he rasped.

She took a deep breath, trying again. 'How long?'

Broad shoulders lifted in a shrug. 'Nine—ten years.'

'Ten years!' Shock made a squeak out of her voice. 'Did—did Shirley know?' she ventured, puzzled, after a moment.

The striking contours of his profile hardened as he made some derisive sound through his nose. 'I doubt very much, pretty... cousin... if the woman you claim was your mother ever actually knew. Or cared,' he appended roughly.

The bitterness in him was tangible enough to make her recoil in her seat. He had been close to Page—far closer than she had ever begun to imagine, she was surprised to realise, sensing the deeply personal grief beneath that tough, impenetrable exterior.

'What happened to him?' she found enough courage to ask at length.

'Do you really care?'

He looked so savage, gripping the wheel with those long dark hands whitening at the knuckles, that she was almost intimidated into silence. But if she wanted him to accept her claim to being a Masterton then she had to start acting like one, she told herself firmly, from somewhere finding the confidence to utter, 'He was my grandfather. I'm interested, that's all.'

'Yes, and that's about the size of it, isn't it?' he tossed angrily back at her. 'Which is why you can sit there nonchalantly talking about a man you never knew without the first bloody idea of the pain he went through—what it's like to suffer!'

His outburst made her flinch. Then she wanted to hurl at him that she knew enough about pain and suffering to last her a lifetime, but that would have revealed too much about herself, so she didn't dare.

'He had a stroke. Now let's forget it,' he said eventually, plunging them both into silence and driving the luxurious car with barely restrained vehemence for the rest of the journey home.

CHAPTER THREE

OVER the next couple of days Alex kept herself occupied by discovering her surroundings. She explored the town, reached from the long road that ran downhill from the house to the quaint and historic seafront which in summer, she knew, would be crowded because of the modern holiday centre with its fun-filled watershoots and garish colours. On the far side of the town, it was, she decided, the only thing to detract from the resort's beauty. Now, though, while waiting for spring to arrive, the town still possessed a sleepy charm, although the waters washing its sandy beach were murky from the silt on this part of the coast, and nothing like the deep blue of the ocean she had become accustomed to in New Zealand.

The Somerset countryside, however, could not be equalled, and, wrapped up in a warm anorak, scarf and gloves, Alex enjoyed ambling alone along the quiet rural lanes and through the silent woods adjacent to Moorlands on tranquillity-restoring walks she remembered Shirley telling her about more than a decade before.

Enjoying herself, though, wasn't the reason for her being here, she reminded herself firmly, no matter how much the moor beckoned or the country lanes offered a diversion from the house and her reluctant awareness of a man she despised and yet who, contrarily, could make her pulses throb with more than just angry resentment whenever she was in his company.

As had happened that morning, when he had left her, to all intents and purposes, browsing through the books in Page's study.

Having caught sight of a photograph sticking out of one of the pigeon-holes in the bureau, she had been so absorbed by other things the bureau had to offer, which included more old photos—mainly of the family, she presumed—as well as some interesting postcards, that she hadn't heard anyone come in until York's voice had cut startlingly through the silence.

'What the hell do you think you're doing?'

Alex started, knocking something off the blotter as she swivelled round on her chair.

'N-nothing,' she uttered inanely. 'I—I saw a photograph I thought was of Shirley and I suppose I just got carried away.'

From the hard cast of his features, he clearly didn't believe her.

'Were you looking for something in particular?'

Alex swallowed, wondering if the dryness in her throat stemmed from guilt or just from his sheer vitality as he stood there in that immaculate grey suit. It was a hard, restless vitality that seemed at odds with the bleak austerity of the room, with its tall mahogany clock and bookcases and the imposing ambience of what had once been his uncle's very private sanctum. But wouldn't he enjoy hurting her if he knew!

'Nothing in particular...'

'Then what were you doing in here under the pretext of looking at books? And what's this?' Casually he fingered the pointed leaf of a potted miniature daffodil she hadn't been able to resist in town the previous afternoon, and which she had placed on a low-standing bookcase just inside the door.

'This place seems so cold. I was just trying to brighten it up a bit,' she defended firmly, and guessed from the way he grimaced as his grey-green eyes scanned the room that he probably agreed with her. But he wouldn't have admitted it in a thousand years, she thought grudgingly, before enquiring with a boldness that refused to be dampened, 'My mother's things...what happened to them?'

An eyebrow lifted sceptically as he came towards her and with one fluid movement picked up the little gold dagger letter-opener that was lying on the rug, placing it back on the desk. 'Do we have them?'

She tried not to breathe, tried not to acknowledge that subtle masculine scent of him that played on her reluctant senses.

'Oh, for heaven's sake, York!' She wasn't going to let him wear her down with suspicion, no matter how much he might try to use that daunting, tyrannical streak to intimidate her. She had come for the letters which Shirley had once told her about in one of her weaker, more confiding moments, and until she found them—if they were here—he could go to hell!

'What sort of things?' he asked then, almost disinterestedly.

Now she had to think quickly. 'Anything. Books. Old toys. Teenage scribblings. You know, girlhood things.'

The clock, indicating the quarter hour, made her jump as it suddenly whirred into motion, as though it were in conspiracy with him to make her more edgy, though she was determined not to let her tension show.

'You're not likely to find anything like that ransacking my uncle's bureau.'

'I hardly expected to! And I wasn't *ransacking*!' she threw back heatedly, her nerves stretched to the limit because of his disturbing proximity. He was standing too close, one immaculately clad arm outstretched, hard knuckles on the edge of the desk.

'As far as I know, my cousin took everything with her when she left, and what she didn't take I would hope Page would have happily burned long ago.' There was nothing but hatred in his voice for his unfortunate cousin—a hatred so intense that it made Alex shudder. 'And to me it looks pretty much as if that's what happened!'

Unconsciously, Alex's fingers gripped the leather cushion under her legs as he made one purposeful move to come and stand, tall and imposing, in front of her.

'What exactly is it you're looking for, Alex?'

'I told you.' She could hear her own voice starting to quiver, and not so much from the threatening quality of his but because she couldn't move, couldn't swivel her chair now without risking actually touching him. 'And I was under the impression I had every right to come in here. Legally if not morally.'

'Morally?' His laugh seemed to split the air. 'What does a conniving little opportunist like you know about morals?'

Animosity burned in his eyes, so intense that involuntarily she shrank back from it, although she managed to keep her head high as he suddenly stooped to rest one hand on the back of her chair, the other on its padded arm.

'My lovely little second cousin didn't have any then— ten years ago—and I'm sure as hell she wouldn't have grown up to stake any ostensible claims to any now. This air of cool poise is out of character, Alex.'

Sudden mockery was etching the dark symmetry of his features with something that was wholly feral and which sent warning bells clamouring through her brain.

'The unrestrained passion of the Alexia I remember wouldn't have diminished with the years. Such elemental attraction makes no concession to time. To age. Or even to hatred.'

His words were intimidatingly soft, the hand above her shoulder dropping now to move with heart-stopping sensuality along the delicate curve of her jaw. His fingers were strong and slightly rough against the heated column of her throat, slipping with outrageous insolence beneath the collar of her blouse, locking her breath in her lungs until she thought she was suffocating.

The clock was silent now, the only sound that steady, somnolent tick, and her expelled breath suddenly shivered through her as she fought a myriad reckless sensations generated by the perverse excitement of his touch. No matter how immune a woman might think she was, that treacherous sexual sophistication of his could break through any resistance, she realised with sudden, terrifying clarity.

'No. Some of us just grow up, York!' she uttered. And with one hard twist of her chair, which had her knocking her knee painfully against his, she leapt up and away from him, out of the room without stopping to subject herself to the mocking triumph she knew would be written on his face.

She was grateful when, the following morning, Celia suggested that they go riding. Not that Alex considered herself a particularly good horsewoman, but she welcomed anything that took her away from the house and York.

'I always try to get in the saddle before I go home as the countryside's so good for riding around here,' Celia commented as she swung the Range Rover into the yard of the pretty moorland stable nestling beneath the dark ochre of the heathland and the lush green hills. Here and there the glint of silver betrayed a stream tumbling down to the wooded valley. 'It keeps the muscles in shape. Not that you need to worry about that,' she said, with an approving glance over Alex's slim figure.

'Even so, I never say no to a workout,' Alex laughed, petting one or two of the equine heads peering curiously out at them above the stable doors as they made their way across the yard.

'York suggested you might enjoy a ride when I told him I was thinking about coming here today,' the woman enlightened her when they were leading their horses out of their respective stalls, Celia looking the part in full riding gear, Alex noted, with an inward grimace at her own rather less suitable anorak and cords.

'Did he?' Fastening the helmet she had hired from the stable, she hoped she had managed to make her voice sound casual. She had heard York drive off in the BMW earlier that morning and had known relief at the likelihood that she might not be seeing him for the rest of the day.

Above them the moor beckoned, open and delightfully wild, and all she wanted to do was canter over the bracken-covered hillside until she reached the top, ride off the tensions that had been plaguing her ever since she had moved into his house. She wanted to forget about York.

When the land had levelled off, though, and they were walking their horses side by side after their first exhilarating canter up through the heath Celia spoke. 'You haven't been hitting it off very well with my son, have you?' was her disconcerting comment. She was flying home later that day, back to Dublin, and Alex was dreading her going, apprehensive about being left entirely alone with York.

She wanted to say, He doesn't believe I'm who I say I am. But she didn't. Apparently, for some reason, York hadn't voiced his concerns about her to his mother, and although Alex didn't imagine Celia Masterton to be a woman easily taken in, the woman had accepted her far more readily than York seemed prepared to do. Better, therefore, she thought, not to start casting doubt in Celia's mind as well!

So she said, 'He obviously resented Shirley for disgracing the family name and running off like she did. I suppose it's only natural, therefore, that he should resent me too.'

'I don't think it's so much that, dear.' They rode on in silence for a few moments before York's mother, looking uncomfortable, went on, 'He loved your grandfather more like a father than an uncle. Unfortunately he was always closer to Page than he was to Kieran, my late husband. And I believe Page—your grandfather—didn't ever really get over...'

Her words were lost, caught and tugged away by the gusty wind that blew up from the wooded valley.

Didn't ever get over what? The stroke? Alex was about to query, but two figures on horseback were trotting towards them from the opposite direction, and her heart missed a beat, every nerve sharpening as she recognised the proud, confident rider sitting astride the dappled stallion. York!

'Well, well, this is an unexpected pleasure!' Cold eyes that appeared green-gold as he brought the prancing stallion to a halt were bright with laughter, skimming cursorily over Alex before coming to rest on his mother. 'I see Kay kept her promise and made sure to reserve the two gentlest horses.'

'Kay being the one on the left,' Celia joked informatively to Alex, who was regarding the small, pretty girl accompanying him with nowhere near the degree of cold interest with which his lovely companion was assessing her.

'I own the stable.' Kay extended a slender gloved hand. 'Well, in partnership with Daddy.' Some years younger than Alex, she spoke with confidence and polish, the short, dark hair cropped neatly into her neck and her figure-hugging jodhpurs and jacket giving her a rather boyish look that somehow added more allure to her femininity.

'York said he had an extra guest,' Kay informed her after the man had introduced them, although he still wasn't committing himself to accepting her as his cousin, Alex noted when he referred to her simply as Alex. 'When he stressed that you might want something gentle, though,' Kay went on, 'I hadn't imagined you to be so young. I thought you'd be more Celia's age. In fact when I saw you coming...' She shrugged, gave a little laugh. 'Oh, well...'

Which is supposed to put me in my place, Alex decided, knowing that Kay was referring to her hair, which flowed beneath the black velour in a riot of bright silver.

'But you obviously had first choice, didn't you, York?' Alex breathed, smiling wryly at the huge beauty of a beast it was obvious only a man of his strength and skill could safely control. 'You certainly picked yourself one hell of a mare!'

'It's a stallion!' Kay uttered indignantly, leaving Alex already regretting allowing herself to stoop to the other woman's level with that *double entendre*, even if it did give her some satisfaction to see the way York's lips firmed, though he made no comment. But then he wouldn't. That iron self-discipline would prevent him from castigating her in public.

Celia was turning her horse's head and Alex did the same, but Celia dropped back to talk to Kay, and to her chagrin Alex found herself riding alongside the stallion.

She hadn't spoken to York alone since that unsettling scene with him in his uncle's study the previous morning and, hiding her discomfort behind a glittering smile, she dropped a glance to his jodhpur-clad leg and said on a derisive little note, 'How's the knee?' She hoped his bruise was twice the size of the one on hers!

His grin was equally derisive. 'As sound as ever—as you're going the right way to finding out.'

He was annoyed, of course, by the way she had spoken to his lady-friend, but, refusing even to acknowledge the sudden throb of tension way down inside her, she returned brittly, 'I'm not seventeen any more, York.'

Just for a second she saw those thick masculine brows knit deeply, could still feel those narrowed eyes studying her, even when she glanced away.

What was he thinking, remembering? A heated flush crept up her throat as she struggled to close her mind against the possibilities. She wanted to canter off, away from him, as far as she could get from this wholly unsettling situation. But that would have been rude. And anyway, there were the others to consider.

They rode in silence for a few moments. Then York asked, 'How does this compare with New Zealand?'

She followed the wide sweep of his arm as it embraced the stretch of hillside tumbling to the isolated woods and grey stone buildings of the stables way below them, aware that he had engineered this meeting, that they hadn't met purely by chance.

'It's colder,' was the first thing that popped into her head. His masculine figure, somehow broadened by the thick cable-knit sweater as he sat astride that magnificent horse, made her feel ridiculously slight and overshadowed on her own, comparatively small pony. But it was a long time since she had been in England and she had only just begun to realise how much she had missed it, and almost inaudibly she whispered, 'It's beautiful,' and knew she hadn't managed to contain her emotion when that gold-green gaze sliced a hard, assessing glance her way.

'What are your plans, Alex?'

She looked at him quickly. 'My plans?'

'Yes.' He shortened his reins, his hands strong and capable as they brought the prancing stallion under control. 'Don't tell me you haven't already plotted quite carefully what you're going to do with my uncle's money. *If* you get your hands on it,' he added grimly.

Unconsciously, Alex lifted her chin, keeping her eyes on the green and purple terrain of the moorland ahead.

'Does that mean you're contesting the will?'

From some distance behind she could hear the voices of the two other women, but they were too far away now to overhear exactly what was being said.

He didn't answer and, with features that looked suddenly pinched, she uttered, 'I told you—you can stick the money!'

'Oh, yes, of course.' His tone implied that her statement was ludicrously unbelievable, and in the stern moment's silence that followed there was only Kay's sudden high-pitched laugh a little way behind them, and the champing of bits, with the moan of the cold, blustery wind that was tugging at them, blowing down from the higher reaches of the moor.

'If I had any need to convince you I was Alexia, I'd hardly have called myself by a different name, would I?' she breathed, grasping at any straw in an almost futile effort to convince him now.

'Why not?' he challenged, unrelenting, winning expertly over the snorting stallion. Its breath made clouds of warm vapour on the air. 'Anyone who was clever enough to understand the teenager with whom I was acquainted would know that she would do exactly that. Shorten her own name and probably take her father's name of Johnson as a deliberate act of rebellion—or an abbreviated form of it, if she wanted to lessen her chances of being traced. And you are clever, Alex.'

But not as clever as you. The thought of his incalculable shrewdness made her shudder.

Suddenly, though, now that they'd turned their horses for home, all her attention was focused on the steep hill they were descending as the pony she was riding, familiar with the homeward trail, took off at a frightening pace.

'Hey, stop!'

She tugged on the reins, tried to remember what one was supposed to do to stop a runaway horse. Ram one's feet hard into the stirrups and push forward? Which would have been all right, she thought, if the ground hadn't been so bumpy and she hadn't completely lost the right stirrup!

Now she was grappling with the reins, bounced precariously to one side before she thought to take her foot out of the other stirrup in an attempt to balance her weight. But the ground underfoot was treacherous—a steep and stony path interspersed with shallow boulders which wouldn't make for a very comfortable landing if she were to fall.

'Felicity! Whoa, girl! Felicity, *stop*!'

Her anxious coaxing was in vain as the mare, reaching more even ground, picked up its pace in a single-minded bid to reach home.

Alex gave a small groan, fear mingling with despair as the moorland seemed to be flying by. How long could she stay on? If she were to be thrown now she could do more damage to herself than it bore thinking about, she realised, her fingers twisting frantically in the flying red mane, until she felt the reins suddenly yanked out of her hands.

The stallion was galloping beside them, and somehow, incredibly, York was controlling the mare, his leg colliding painfully with Alex's as, after a few scary moments, he brought the creature to a snorting and protesting halt.

She would have fallen then, onto the hard ground, if York hadn't been there to prevent it, but instead, with his arm to support her, she merely slid down his leg to land on her feet, shaken but otherwise unhurt.

'Well, that's one way to get out of answering any awkward questions.'

She was trembling as he dismounted, her voice shaky as she countered, 'I'm not that stupid.' But she knew, despite his cynical remark, that he was conscious that it hadn't been something she had deliberately set out to do.

'Are you all right?'

His quiet concern, so at variance with his usual hostility towards her, made her almost want to weep with relief—relief that she was still in one piece at any rate. But all she said was, 'I haven't broken my neck, if that's what you were hoping.'

'Not a bit of it,' he drawled, that lean, chiselled face etched with cold, hard mockery. 'Otherwise it would deprive me of being able to do it myself.'

'Very funny,' she retorted, climbing back onto the mare which he was still holding, even though her legs felt like jelly.

'Are you sure you don't want me to hold onto the reins for a while?' he offered, though without any trace of mockery now, after she had grabbed them from him rather ungraciously.

'No,' she said flatly, more bravely than she felt, because she could hear the others riding up behind them and at that moment she couldn't face Kay's silent ridicule. And the woman *would* ridicule her, laugh inwardly, Alex was sure, because she couldn't even handle a docile mare!

'What happened?' The question came in unison, Kay sounding a little offhanded, Celia concerned, as they drew level with her and York.

Go on—tell them! Alex dared him silently, guessing that he would probably relish the chance of embarrassing her by telling them the truth.

'Nothing we couldn't handle,' he relayed casually, swinging himself lithely back onto the stallion.

'Thanks,' Alex murmured, surprised, as he leaned forward to adjust his seat, softly enough so that the others didn't have to hear.

'Forget it,' he said dismissively, urging his horse to walk on, and she wasn't sure whether he was referring to saving her from some unthinkable injury, or to preventing her from appearing an utter fool in front of Kay.

CHAPTER FOUR

'I'M DRIVING up to Bristol,' York informed Alex the next morning, looking stupendous in a silver-grey suit and immaculate white shirt as she met him coming down the stairs. 'I'm doing an outside TV interview on the new site we're developing up there and I want you with me,' he told her peremptorily.

'Why? Nervous about speaking to the camera on your own?' she couldn't help quipping in response.

A censuring lift of an eyebrow assured her he was not amused.

Well, why should he be nervous? she thought. He'd look good on television and handle it superbly. As he handled everything, she couldn't help thinking resentfully. He just wanted her with him because he didn't trust her in his house now that Celia had gone!

'Give me five minutes,' she said, fancying a drive to Bristol and therefore curbing the strong desire to protest against his lordly attitude. Her back stiffened nevertheless as he passed her with that air of clean, fresh vitality surrounding him and muttered, having the last word, 'Make that three.'

The site was for a massive office complex on the fringe of the city, and there was an air of excitement around the newly completed section of the development where the cameras had been set up.

'It must make you feel very proud to think that this is your baby,' Alex was unable to help remarking as they picked their way with the site manager through rubble and dust outside the tastefully designed pale stone and glass construction. 'Well, your company's, anyway.'

'I think satisfied is more the word.' Beneath a yellow hard hat—compulsory on site—York's head lifted with the emotion he had spoken of, his eyes scanning the finished section of phase one of the building work. Strong, magnificent and somehow beautiful, he was as much a perfect specimen of man as the building he was admiring was a tribute to modern architecture, Alex thought, and, strangely, felt a tightening sensation in her throat. 'There was a lot of controversy about whether we were right to proceed but we managed to please both the planners and the environmentalists in the end.'

'That's a feat in itself!' she laughed. She too was wearing a protective hat, which didn't do much for the dog-tooth check jacket and straight skirt which she was wearing as the weather had suddenly turned spring-like that morning. But why did she feel so much more at ease with him out here—away from the house? Was it because she felt so much more on an equal footing with him anyway from Moorlands? Less threatened? Less of an intruder? 'If you knew the obstacles one developer met with down under, you'd never believe it.'

'Oh, I would! Believe me, I would!' he assured her with an ironical twist of his mouth. 'Start putting in plans for anything and no one can see anything beyond the profit you're going to make.'

'Which in Mastertons' case is next to—' Nothing, she had been about to jest, but at that moment stumbled over a cable and, to a chorus of apologies from several of the film crew, found herself caught firmly in York's steadying arms.

'Look where you're going,' he breathed admonishingly against her hair, and beneath the pounding of a steam-hammer on another part of the site she thought he sounded rather breathless.

'I'm all right.' For an endless moment it seemed that she was caught against his hard strength—a moment when she recognised the heat of something fierce and darkly enigmatic in his eyes before she was released, her knees feeling as wobbly as blancmange.

'Sorry about that, Mr Masterton.' They knew him, of course, Alex realised of the young cameramen who were quickly pulling their cables out of harm's way. But then, he exuded that air of power and authority without even trying, she thought, and, when she found herself still trembling from the chaos his nearness had caused in her, decided she had to be mad to have even considered coming here.

The film crew had grabbed his attention now, though, and with the interviewer—a red-headed young woman in a chic green suit—they were suggesting, above the din of a pneumatic drill that had also started up, how they would like the filming to go.

'We're going to do the interview with the councillor first and then perhaps we could have about two minutes of your time, Mr Masterton.'

Their deference to him was unquestionable, and with a small inward sigh Alex leaned against the cool marble of a newly constructed pillar, glad of a few moments to regain her composure.

'Alex! Alex Johns!'

Her moment of recovery was short-lived, shattered by a voice she recognised and instantly wished she hadn't.

'Lonnie?'

Stockily built, with dark hair, and a swagger that came from being far too good-looking, Lonnie Burrowes still sported that air of self-importance that Alex had once mistaken for maturity. He was a jumped-up journalist she had first met in an Auckland office nine years ago and who, she knew, had returned to his native England eventually. But to turn up here—of all places!

'What a small world. Fancy running into the lovely Miss Johns here.' There was nothing complimentary in his use of the word 'lovely'. Lonnie enjoyed hurting people if there was a story in it. And boy, did he have the means to hurt her!

'Fancy!' She forced herself to smile, a whole host of emotions causing a painful tightening in her stomach. He was, after all, the only person she could have done without running into, the one person who could do a lot of harm if he found out that she was calling herself Masterton. And it wasn't as if he wouldn't want to do harm. He had asked her out once and she'd refused because she didn't like his professional ethics—the way he obtained his information—and he'd never forgiven her for that.

'You didn't come with *him*, did you?' To say he knew who York was was an understatement, Alex thought, and from his disbelieving glance in the man's direction he looked both impressed and bewildered. 'He's not a boyfriend, surely?'

She could sense Lonnie's mouth watering for any tasty morsel of information he could get his teeth into, and a little shiver ran down her spine.

'Hardly,' she breathed, pulling a face, trying to conceal her discomfiture at running into him.

'You work for him?'

Alex didn't answer. Let him believe it if he wanted to.

'Are you living here now, then?' he enquired, and as he moved nearer she could smell the cloying thickness of his aftershave lotion. And when she nodded he prompted, 'In Bristol?'

She shook her head. 'More in Somerset.' She was watching every word she said.

'How long have you been in the UK?'

She shrugged. 'A little while.'

He could tell she was being cagey, his full lips curling knowingly as he sent a sideways glance towards York. 'We must get together some time.'

Alex's insides were repelled at the thought of any sort of liaison with Lonnie Burrowes. 'I don't think so.' One hint of what she was doing here and he might decide to print everything he knew ... 'I'm so busy,' she appended quickly, reminding herself that it wouldn't do to alienate him altogether. 'I really don't think it's going to be possible...'

She tried to sound half-sorry, and felt her heart sink as York drawled from behind, 'What isn't going to be possible, little cousin?'

Alex's stomach seemed to tighten into knots. Why did he have to call her that in front of Lonnie Burrowes? Why? When he didn't even believe it himself? Did he imagine that if threatened with exposure to the newspapers she might climb down and admit to being a fraud? she thought despairingly, the arm he placed around her shoulders in mock-affection nevertheless causing her pulses to leap like skittish colts.

'Your *cousin*?' Lonnie's mouth had popped open in stark surprise. Those bright blue eyes were narrowing, however, as that journalistic brain was already assessing that there could be even more to it than that. 'I thought you didn't have any family. That's what you told me...' His voice tailed off, puzzled, pondering, and, too conscious of that masculine arm around her shoulders, Alex grew tense and hot.

'Did she, by Jove?' York's tone alone willed her to look at him. 'Why on earth did you do that?' His amusement concealed raw sarcasm—that smile he gave her solely for Lonnie's benefit—but Alex could feel his bunching muscle in the hard steel of his arm.

'I meant parents and siblings—brothers and sisters,' she bluffed quickly, rather than risk letting Lonnie think that she had been deliberately trying to hide something from him, and she flashed York a brilliant smile which was repaid with an almost painful tightening of those fingers on her arm.

'Your cousin, eh?' Lonnie's appetite was whetted and he was salivating like a dog with a new bone. He didn't believe it. That much was obvious. He was hoping for something tastier, she could tell. He was looking from one to the other. 'I don't see much family resemblance.'

'Probably because we aren't related,' York conveyed tersely.

'Not related?' Lonnie frowned, looking at Alex. 'But you just said—'

'Only by marriage. York's father was adopted. Therefore we're only step-cousins,' Alex was forced to explain. 'If there is such a thing.'

Lonnie's sickly smile returned. 'How convenient,' he commented, savouring the news.

'Not half as convenient as you'll find having a job was if you try and make something out of it!' York threatened, seeming instantly to have assessed the type of man they were dealing with. 'I wouldn't try to pretend any affection for newspapermen in general, but it's your type of sleazy journalism, Burrowes, that gives the rest of your lot a bad name.'

So he knew who Lonnie was, Alex thought, breathing more easily as York removed his arm from her shoulders, while the other man seemed to shrink beneath York's inimical glare.

'No love for the journalist, eh?' Thick-skinned as ever, Lonnie wasn't allowing York's threat to intimidate him for long. 'But obviously there are exceptions—when you snuggle up to the hottest thing down under with an eye for a scoop!'

Though the early-spring sunshine was actually pleasant where they were standing in the shelter of the new building, a chill ran shudderingly through Alex. The suspicion she had seen in York's eyes every time he looked at her was now one of such tangible strength that she felt it pressing against her like a physical force.

His eyes turning glacial now, he started to say something, but the producer was calling, 'OK, Mr Masterton! Ready when you are!' and Alex was relieved when, with one look that seemed to dissect her, York strode off to prepare himself for the interview.

'What did I say? Didn't you tell him you used to work for a newspaper? Quite a dark horse, aren't you, keeping things to yourself?'

There was only malicious curiosity behind Lonnie's remarks, and Alex's stomach churned with raw, sickening fear. Things were complicated enough without Lonnie turning up and threatening to...to what? She couldn't bear to consider just how impossible he could make life for her here in England if he chose to.

'Why don't you take a dive? Preferably into a deep quarry!' she breathed as anger finally overcame her fears, keeping her voice down so that no one else would hear.

Lonnie merely chuckled. 'One of Masterton's?' he suggested quietly, with a toss of his head towards York, who was just out of earshot, having a microphone fitted to an immaculate lapel. 'I suppose letting on you worked for a profession he clearly hates wouldn't do much to increase your chances with him, would it?' he remarked outrageously. And then he added, 'Correct me if I'm wrong, but I'd say you've really got the hots for him, haven't you?' He sneered.

Alex knew his conjecture was only strengthened when she felt his eyes assess the colour that was surging into her face.

'And you've got a one-track mind,' she spat, grateful that a member of the television crew was on hand to silence any further comment by Lonnie, and she turned away as the interview with the councillor was about to begin.

After that it was York's turn, and Alex couldn't help thinking how his television presence far outclassed the other man's.

The item wasn't live, but it was for the national network. York, though, appeared nerveless in contrast to his colleague—a fidgety little man with glasses—but he would have come over well even without the other man's shortcomings to emphasise his enviable confidence. He could even have given the interviewer a lesson in cool collectedness, Alex realised, deciding that the young woman's mind was clearly more on York than it was on her interview. And when this is over, she thought with a little shiver of unease, he's going to take me apart—again!

Lonnie had gone by the time the interviews were finished.

York was silent, the grim set of his mouth assuring Alex of his dark mood as she hurried to keep up with his long strides for the short distance to the car. Nor was he very communicative as he negotiated the busy city traffic, but when they were on the motorway, heading west again, he said, 'So you're a reporter. Is programme researcher a fancy new name for it these days?'

In the outside lane, they had to be doing over eighty, but he hadn't needed to raise his voice. The car was adequately soundproofed, cruising as smoothly as a dream.

She was about to remark that her job description was exactly what it said it was but he didn't give her the chance.

'Exactly who are you?' he demanded, his eyes narrowing as he sliced a glance in her direction.

'You know who I am,' she breathed, cursing Lonnie for instilling further doubt in York's mind.

'So what are you doing here? Looking for some dirt to dig up about the family?'

She uttered a nervous little laugh, watching him through lowered lashes. 'Why, York?' she murmured, her voice unintentionally sultry yet taunting. 'Is there something to dig up?'

The hardening lines around his mouth should have warned her that she was challenging the wrong man, but she had to go on—not for her own sake but for Shirley's. Poor, lost, unfortunate Shirley. 'You must admit it *would* make interesting reading, wouldn't it, York?' Her tone was strung with biting cynicism. 'Why Page disowned his only daughter. And why his nephew's now refusing to acknowledge hers.'

'I'm warning you...' he rasped. 'Just like I warned that filth-raking friend of yours...'

'Oh, *please*!' she uttered emphatically. 'Don't bracket us together! He was just someone I worked with in New Zealand years ago when I had designs on becoming a journalist. Anyway, I never actually took the position officially.'

'Why not? Did you have too much of a conscience?' Contempt trickled thickly through his words.

Something like that, she thought, but didn't say as much, which didn't help to improve his opinion of her. He went on, 'What are you—in some league with the rat that he should turn up in the very place where we happened to be this morning? What is it you want, Alex? Some glorious revenge for Shirley? If that's the case, then don't waste your time. She was hardly worth it!'

His flaying remark seemed to leave her skin bloodless for a moment, her face appearing pale and gaunt within the silvery frame of her hair. But, recovering herself, she whipped back at him, 'Oh, for heaven's sake! I hadn't arranged to be there this morning! You invited me—correction!—ordered me to come, remember? I wish to goodness now I hadn't bothered! And that goes for coming to this infernal country as well!'

Controlling her temper was an effort, the strain of which brought her ridiculously close to tears, but determinedly she fought back the emotion. She would never, never cry in front of this man.

He switched the radio on then, very quietly—a silent indication that for now he had stopped riding roughshod over her.

After a while the programme of classical music which he had selected helped soothe her frayed nerves and her temper, restoring her equilibrium after that unsettling and unwelcome meeting with Lonnie.

They made amazingly good time to the motorway exit and the fringes of Exmoor, but instead of heading straight back to the house York took them on a scenic drive over the moor.

A short, blustery burst of raindrops sent a spattering of silver across the windscreen—a light spring shower, over almost as soon as it had begun.

The road was hilly, dropping away steeply on the right to verdant pasture and the sea. Sheep roamed freely on the grass verges of the road, ignoring them, nipping delicately at the short green roots. The sudden sighting of a male pheasant brought a pleasurable exclamation from Alex, its purple and copper plumage unmistakable as it darted out from behind a thick clump of gorse, so that York had to brake hard, those reflexes razor-sharp.

'Do you drive?' he asked, but casually, as if he were speaking to a stranger, as he took a left turning, proceeding down into a deep and plunging wooded valley.

'Yes. But not like a maniac,' she said.

The look he gave her was wry, amused. 'You think I drive like a maniac?'

'No.' I think you drive superbly, she thought, but didn't say it, silently admiring the confidence with which he had brought them swiftly but safely down the M5 into the comparative peace of the Somerset countryside.

'I thought that while you're here in this "infernal country",' he said, reminding her of what she now regretted as a rather childish and unnecessary loss of control earlier, 'you might like to see some of its livelier high spots.' But he was only joking. This place was breathtaking—a steep descent overlooking lush fields that rose to the gorse and heather-covered slopes of the moor.

York's window was open and one could almost touch the silence beyond it. Silence, save for the purr of the car's engine and the plaintive, quivering voices of the sheep with their new lambs, specks of fluffy white against the green hills.

'Oh, look!' Something was moving down in the damp field just below them, and, craning her neck to see out of the driver's window, excitedly Alex pointed to the solitary brown shape of a hare.

> 'All things that love the sun are out of doors...
> The grass is bright with rain-drops; on the moors
> The hare is running races in her mirth...'

The seat belt tugged painfully across her breasts as York suddenly braked hard. A lapse in concentration that was totally out of character had brought them too close to the hedge on the sharp, right-hand bend, she realised, surprised.

> 'And with her feet she from the plashy earth
> Raises a mist...'

York's voice tailed off as he finished the line of poetry she had started. 'Where did you learn that?' He sounded strangely hoarse.

Alex pursed her lips, thinking. 'I've known it for ever. Why?'

'Just that I hadn't imagined you'd be the type of woman to like poetry—much less Wordsworth,' he commented, which had to account for his voice being somehow accusingly soft just now.

She bit back an obvious retort to say only, 'And I could have said the same thing about you.'

His lips formed a wry half-smile as he drove them down into the valley, over a small stone bridge spanning a stream. A little further on a tiny stone church stood in quiet solemnity on their left.

'One can't avoid it at Moorlands. The library's crammed with it. Wordsworth. Byron. Shakespeare.'

'Not at the moment,' she admitted a little self-consciously. And, catching his questioning glance, she added, 'Byron and Shakespeare are in my room.'

She could feel his eyes on her briefly but she didn't look his way, couldn't tell what was going on behind that intellectual study.

'I don't know whether I should commiserate with or envy them,' he drawled.

She didn't answer—partly because she couldn't think of anything to say, but partly because something in that last remark reminded her of how dangerously aware of him she was becoming.

Suddenly then, as the road descended again between banks of high hedges, he asked, 'Are you familiar with *Lorna Doone*?'

'Not personally,' she quipped, endeavouring to ease her own tension, and tagged on more seriously, 'I read it once—a long time ago.'

That strong chin jerked upwards. 'She was supposedly married in that church back there.'

Alex glanced back, her hair falling softly over her shoulder. Of course. Oare Church. This whole valley was named after her.

'Didn't she have a cruel, autocratic cousin?' she wasn't unable to stop herself remarking.

The jibe was only acknowledged in a slight tightening of those long hands on the wheel. 'Yes. He shot her— while she was in the act of marrying another man.'

Something in his voice sent a sudden and unexpected ache of desolation through her. 'Is that what you've got lined up for me?' she enquired poignantly.

He laughed now as he steered the powerful car over another tiny bridge with only inches to spare on either side. On York's side she could see the ford through which they could have driven, swollen with the winter rain. There was a riding stable here too, and, opposite, a gift shop, still closed for the winter season. A much visited beauty spot in summer, Alex realised, preferring the valley as it was now. Totally isolated. Lorna Doone's own.

'What would you prefer I did?' he enquired after a while, when they had left the ford and the quaint little buildings behind them. 'Married you myself and gave you the lesson in basic scruples you sorely deserve?'

He was slowing down suddenly, pulling off into a lay-by where trees formed a canopy overhead and tall ferns sheltered them from any passing traffic.

As she heard the ominous click of the handbrake, Alex's tongue seemed to stick to the roof of her mouth.

'Forgive me for sounding hackneyed,' she uttered tremulously, peeved by his last remark about her scruples, 'but I wouldn't marry you if you were the last man on earth.'

His smile was unperturbed. 'Not in the true sense of the word perhaps but...'

She saw the intent in his eyes as he leaned her way, and she swallowed to dislodge the lump she could feel just below her windpipe. 'Don't you dare,' she breathed. But his smile merely widened.

'Come on... Alex...' His voice—his eyes—mocked. 'You've found yourself wanting a man you despise, and it isn't in your plan of things, whatever that may be, is it, darling? It's a complication you didn't want—but there all the same.'

Wasn't that the very thought she'd had herself? she thought, panic leaping in her eyes as he bent towards her. She put up both hands to try to hold him at bay, but with a soft laugh under his breath he caught her to him and she thought she heard him groan as his mouth obliterated the small protest that rose from hers.

His kiss was nothing like that gentle yet calculated act when he had been testing her responses that first day back at Moorlands. This time the hard insistence of his mouth seemed to be annihilating her common sense, sending desire through her that was as wild as the moor, as restless and abandoned as the stream she could hear gurgling somewhere close by and which fed the river and gave life to the land, because that was what his kiss was doing to her—giving her life.

She didn't want to resist him, to refuse herself the pleasure that she knew his lips and hands would be capable of giving her, that even on the other side of the world—devouring those articles about him—she had sometimes imagined...

She blotted it out of her mind, only the actuality of what was happening bringing her surging against him now, and as her mouth parted in almost hungry desperation she thought, Dear heaven, I want this! I want *him*!

His lips were warm against her throat and she lifted her head to allow them access to the pulsing hollow just above the V of her blouse, her lashes lowered, her eyes revelling in the blurred vision of his dark flesh, the darker sweep of his lashes. The rhythm of his breathing seemed to match the thundering need raging through her blood.

Trembling, her hands slid the length of his broad back, slipping beneath his jacket. She felt the muscle tauten at his waist, heard his angry rasp of wanting before he jerked his head up again.

'What the devil are you doing here? What *are* you?' He looked like some primeval warring god, his face almost savage with need and frustration, as roughly he caught the soft platinum hair at the back of her head, twisting it round his fingers as though he wanted to twist the truth out of her.

'You're hurting me,' she groaned, half-afraid of that roused masculine anger.

'You like me hurting you,' he taunted, locking her hair more securely round his hand. 'You wouldn't have dared to come here if you didn't. You seem to know enough about me to realise that despite my attempts to find Alexia I wouldn't have welcomed her with meek acceptance or with open arms. Verbally or otherwise...' His lips were almost dangerously tender against one corner of her swollen mouth. 'You're a glutton for punishment, Alex.'

'No,' she denied in a feeble voice.

'Yes,' he breathed, and this time when his mouth covered hers his kiss was imperative and unrelenting, demanding an acknowledgement of everything he had said.

She didn't even try to resist him—couldn't—because, no matter what her mind tried to dictate, her body had a will of its own, responding to him with a need that craved its own domination. And when his hand slid inside her blouse, cupping the lace-covered flesh in his warm palm, she couldn't do anything but permit that as well, the small, guttural sound she made in her throat seeming to echo his deep sigh of satisfaction as he cradled the silken warmth of her flesh.

'You see . . . Alex . . . you're a masochist,' he breathed. 'You delight in your own subjugation.'

He lifted his head to look down into her slumberous eyes, watching with cold-blooded mockery the way her pupils dilated as he fondled the aching fullness of her breast.

'But you're not immune to me, are you, York?' Her voice was trembling from the torturous ecstasy of his calculated caresses. It was no use denying it and, trying to save face, she spat out, 'You hate yourself because you want me.' His callous mockery made her laugh out loud in nervous defiance. 'A woman you don't even like! Can't even trust!'

His expression was sardonic. 'Then we're both slaves to our most primitive instincts, aren't we, darling?' he accepted, his lips nipping her throat with sensuous treachery although his words were overlaid with a raw emotion that seemed to drag his breath through his lungs.

Oh, to see him vulnerable, helpless, as engulfed by desire and shame as that foolish little teenager who had stumbled out of his room with her pride in tatters—to hear him begging, the way Shirley had begged him . . .

She shut her eyes against the images the thoughts induced, repelled by them, silently sympathising with the older woman's inescapable susceptibility to him. The only thing that had driven a wedge between mother and daughter . . .

He lifted his head again as he heard her shuddering sigh, and, as if he could read her thoughts, he murmured softly, 'Alex or Alexia—or whatever you want to call yourself—for whatever reason you're here, you're not going to escape with your pride intact—you know that, don't you?'

'Neither are you,' she promised softly, her gaze fixed on the plush tan leather of the dashboard so he wouldn't see how much his sensual threat intimidated her, but he merely laughed and, pulling away from her, left her fumbling with the buttons of her blouse and restarted the car.

CHAPTER FIVE

ALEX wasn't sure whether York intended to carry out the sensual threat he had issued that day in the Lorna Doone valley, or if it had been merely a ploy to scare her off, but during the days that followed, while she continued her search, she did her utmost to keep out of his way.

She wanted to leave Moorlands, leave England, get as far away as she possibly could from York and his terrifying influence over her. But she still hadn't found what she was looking for, and she had no intention of leaving Moorlands, having subjected herself to its owner's smouldering animosity for nothing. Because York was, and would always be, sole owner, she had already thoroughly resolved; although it was well within her power to claim the inheritance Page had left his granddaughter, York was right to think that she had no right to it, and there was no way her conscience could justifiably allow her to pursue a claim she could never be truly entitled to, even as retribution for Shirley.

She spent a couple of days on a sightseeing trip in London. This was a holiday of sorts, after all. And she was glad that York's work was to take him away for another couple of days and—much to his reluctance, she felt—he had to leave her alone at the house. He threatened her with the housekeeper's vigilance before he left.

Joyce Stern, the ageless divorcée who had been running the house for thirty years or more, was frighteningly efficient and tended to live up to her name, and Alex wondered if Shirley had been intimidated by her.

'Her and Page and you!' she railed, having voiced her suspicions to York as she watched him pick up his briefcase in the hall.

He laughed at the angry spots of colour in her cheeks, the guarded expression in her eyes as he swung back to her.

'You forget, I was still only a boy when my cousin decided to leave home,' he said smoothly, reminding her. 'Nevertheless, it's comforting to know that I've gained another, and that when I come back she'll still be waiting for me.' His kiss was an insult, a mockery of everything he had said, and so swift that it might not have happened but for the pounding at her temples, the upsurge of traitorous desire that stalked like a demon through her blood.

The day after he left, she took a stroll into town and, after doing some shopping, wandered down as far as the old harbour.

The weather was growing milder by the day. The tide was out, and the sun was reflecting off the glass and metalwork of the moored boats sitting there on the glistening mud in the little marina which was protected from the sea by the ancient stone of the harbour wall. It was clear enough today to see across the channel to the Welsh hills, and, finding a quaint little tea-room opposite the harbour, Alex sat enjoying the view over a cup of coffee and a Danish pastry before starting on the long trek home.

She was almost out of town, climbing the hill up to the house, when she heard a car horn beep loudly behind her.

The red saloon pulled up and Lonnie was grinning out at her.

'Want a lift?' he called through the open passenger door.

Alex's spirits sank. 'The idea was to get some exercise,' she said tartly, disinclined to get into his car.

'Don't be such a stick-in-the-mud. Hop in,' he insisted.

Well, what harm could it do really? she thought, complying, not wishing to find herself on the wrong side of Lonnie Burrowes.

He looked satisfied as he drove up the hill, past the few smart urban houses that climbed with it. He was casually dressed, as she was, in a thick sweater and jeans.

'Hasn't that cousin of yours bought you a car yet? Or are you doing your bit for the environment by walking everywhere?' He laughed as he cast her a more than interested glance that made her skin prickle. The truth was that she could have used the Range Rover if she had wanted to. She just didn't feel inclined to take anything more from York than she had to, that was all.

'Tell me where.'

They had come to the top of the hill, almost opposite the house.

'It's all right. I can walk from here,' she told him, keen to get out, already reaching for the doorhandle.

'Nonsense. I'll take you all the way,' he said, insistent again, and, quick to spot the direction of her gaze, pulled across the junction and onto the beech-hemmed drive, murmuring, 'Chance would be a fine thing.'

Alex cringed. Some women would probably welcome his innuendoes. He was thrusting, ambitious and handsome. Some women. But not her.

'Exactly what are you doing down here, Lonnie?'

He was steering the car around the grassy island where the maple tree stood. New shoots had started to appear on its gnarled branches during the past week.

'I had to see someone in Lynmouth and thought I'd pop in to see you on my way back. I was hoping—Holy...!' The obscenity, at his first sight of Moorlands, was unrepeatable and he braked, dumbstruck, admiring the house.

'If you had a home like this, what the hell were you doing in a modest little flat in New Zealand? Why did you lead me to believe you didn't have any family? Because you did, you know, no matter what you said in front of *him* on that building site the other day. Why didn't you tell me you were Alexia Masterton, related to the biggest name in building and quarrying in this country? And while we're on that subject, why were you calling yourself Johns? You weren't old enough to have been married when I first knew you—'

'There were reasons,' she said quickly, her gaze straying to the house behind the low walls draped in ivy, to the paler tones of the stone around its leaded windows, and the familiar ball on top of the central part of the edifice between the two wings. 'I wanted my independence,' she went on, picking her words carefully. 'It was difficult to find my own identity...' she gave a little laugh, though she was feeling anything but light-hearted '...coming from a place like this.'

Bringing the car through the entrance to the courtyard, Lonnie gave a snort of disbelief.

'That isn't the reason why.' He was looking at her suspiciously, at the dark, guarded expression in her eyes. 'You never lived here at all, did you? I did some checking. No one knows who you are—or even what you look like. Alexia Masterton, who disappeared off the face of the earth just after her eighteenth birthday. Just after old man Masterton's rather dubious daughter took that overdose. And now his granddaughter magically returns, not only to England, but to the home she never knew!

'My editor would pay a lot for a story like that—where you've been all these years, why you disappeared. You might even get some crank saying you aren't her, which could start some unscrupulous bastard delving a bit too deep for comfort. But you keep them guessing, sweetheart...' His fingers lifted to caress her cheek but she shrank away from them as if they were live filaments. 'Keep them guessing, and I promise they'll never get the truth from me.'

Alex looked at him, blue eyes still wary. What was he saying?

'Why not?' she challenged, cursing the day when, friendless and unhappy, she had been naïve enough to befriend a man like Lonnie Burrowes. 'I would have thought you wouldn't have wanted to hesitate at taking a snipe at me.'

He gave a good imitation of looking hurt. 'Now that isn't fair! Anyway, betraying your trust is hardly likely to earn me the chance of seeing you again.'

So that's what he still wants. Me, she thought, repelled.

'Thanks for the lift.' Swiftly she was out of the car and slamming the door, aware that Lonnie was shaking his head and laughing as he turned the car, screaming back down the drive. He pulled to a sudden halt just by the entrance, waving exuberantly through his open window. Then he screeched out of the gates a mere second before York swung in, and she could tell by the speed at which he pulled up on the cobbles a moment later that he wasn't very pleased.

'What the hell was he doing here?' He caught up with her before she even reached the porch. 'Is that the sort of company you bring into this house when I'm not around?'

He had obviously seen Lonnie wave to her as though they were the best of friends—or worse, she thought, cringing, which was probably, she guessed, what Lonnie had wanted him to think.

Angry with him, and with herself for letting him upset her to the point that she was actually shaking, she bit back, 'Think what you like. I didn't invite him here!'

'I don't care whether you did or you didn't! I won't have him snooping around here while I'm away. You're to tell him he isn't welcome here, is that clear? And while you're about it, tell him, if he must drive like an imbecile, not to leave his rubber all over my drive!'

She followed his angry gesture to the tracks left like scars on the gravel. Like the scars etched deep inside her, she couldn't help comparing bitterly.

Thinking better of reminding him that it wasn't entirely *his* drive, she wanted to fling back that she despised Lonnie Burrowes—that she didn't want him anywhere near her. And then, just for one weak moment, that dominating force and strength of character that gave York such an edge over the other man made her want to cry out to him, Oh *help* me—please!

But, if her wounds were exposed to him, she knew that he—more than anyone else—would derive the most satisfaction from hurting her.

'Tell him yourself!' she flung over her shoulder as she turned to go into the house, only to be disconcerted when several long strides brought his powerful figure level with her again.

'What's wrong, Alex?' He clicked his tongue disapprovingly. 'Boyfriend making you snappy?'

He isn't my boyfriend! she almost hurled back, but decided it wasn't worth the breath, and as she started through the door in front of him she glanced back at him to murmur, 'What's wrong, York? Jealous?'

If she had been trying to provoke him, which she hadn't, she couldn't have succeeded more efficiently, and she gasped as hard fingers caught her arm, dragging her back into the fierce clutches of his anger.

'Jealous? Why should I be jealous,' he snarled, 'when I know I could take you upstairs and have you to myself for the rest of the afternoon? That any man could have you—'

The crack that rang through the porch and the wide hallway made her realise that she had struck that hard cheek. She stared numbly up at the imprint of her hand on his face, changing now from white to red, and fearfully she saw rage darken his eyes before he muttered softly, through clenched teeth, 'Have you quite finished?'

He looked like some wild Gaelic gypsy, black hair falling forward, the dark blood of his forebears pulsing through his veins like savage fire.

'Have you?' she seethed acidly. Whipped raw by his remark, and yet shamed by the loss of control it had prompted in her, she swept away from him, smarting even more from the self-basing knowledge that at least part of what he had said to her was probably right.

She was reading, curled up with her legs under her in the large, sunny lounge, when he strode in carrying a couple of cardboard boxes later that afternoon. She knew he had been clearing out the loft.

'Here. You wanted to know if there were any of Shirley's things still around,' he reminded her, dumping the boxes down onto the expensive carpet in front of her. 'Try sorting through that lot,' he said, and strode out again, ignoring her small exclamation of surprise.

Keenly, Alex discarded her book to do as he'd advised. The boxes were very old and dusty, and so was most of what was in them. Magazines. A broken toy. A watch that didn't work. Zealously, she sifted through it all, pausing now and again when something of interest caught her eye. The beginnings of a poem. The odd scribbled letter.

When York came back some time later, everything had been carefully replaced, save for an old battered teddy still lying on the floor.

'Is this all there is?' Alex looked up at York from where she was kneeling beside one of the boxes. There was a grimy smudge halfway down her left cheek. 'Is this it?'

He grimaced. 'Isn't that enough? My cousin hasn't lived here for the past twenty-odd years. What more did you expect?'

Silently, she got up, rubbing her leg to ease the pins and needles that had come from kneeling too long. As he'd said, what more could she expect?

'What do you want me to do with it all?' he queried as, after taking one look at her grimy hands, she made a move towards the door.

Alex shrugged. 'Dispose of it,' she said tonelessly.

'What?' He looked dubious. '*All* of it?'

'Yes.' She could hardly take it all back to New Zealand with her, could she?

'Are you sure?'

'Do I have to spell it out?' she enquired pointedly, fixing him with a look that defied challenging, unaware of how a gradual weariness that had been coming on all day had made her sound cross and unconcerned.

'No, I think you've made it plain enough.' He moved towards the sad spectacle of dusty boxes—all that remained as testimony to someone's life and somehow incongruous in the bright, immaculate lounge. 'No keepsakes? Nothing that means enough to you that you might just want to hang onto it?' He was looking at her obliquely, his strong, lean features harsh, judgemental. 'Not a glimmer of emotion, Alex? Or would that be expecting too much over someone as obviously as uncaring as my cousin was?'

She stood there saying nothing, feeling like an emotional punch bag for his verbal brutality. The truth was that going through the woman's things had pierced her more acutely than her pride would ever let her show. It was an all too painful reminder of a wasted life, of someone who had allowed circumstances to destroy her totally. Regret was a deep ache in her breast as she turned away again. She was in no mood to have a slanging match with York.

'You've forgotten to put this in with the rest of the garbage.'

She flinched from his deliberately cutting description of Shirley's worthless belongings and, glancing back, saw him scooping up the forlorn little bear.

'Why did you leave this out? Thinking of keeping it for your own babies?' His tone mocked her and quickly she moved across, snatched it out of his hand. He looked even more amused. 'Do you like babies, Alex? Or are you one of these women who wouldn't dream of allowing anyone to see her getting even remotely maternal?'

She clutched the bear tightly to her, her face indignant. 'That's none of your business!'

He laughed at the colour she could feel burning her cheeks. 'I would have said it was very much my business, the procreation of future Masterton heirs.'

'Even bogus ones?' she jeered.

He tilted his head to one side, his mouth firming as though he was considering her point.

'But they wouldn't be bogus if I sired them, now would they?' he suggested softly, moving towards her, so that Alex felt as if her breathing had suddenly seized up.

'I suppose you think that's funny!' Why did her voice have to shake, turn traitor on her and remind him of her shameful and reluctant awareness of him?

'Not at all.' His smile was a cynical movement of lips. 'There could be something rather challenging in taming you, Alex. In discovering a woman whose background is rather an enigma, to say the least.'

'Like yours, you mean?' she threw back, forcing herself to ignore that molten slick of excitement thickening in her veins at the thought of just what he might possibly have in mind for her.

He made a dismissive sound through his nostrils. 'Oh, there's nothing at all mysterious about mine. If your memory needs refreshing, my father was legally adopted by Page's after his first wife—your great-grandmother—died, when my father was only two years old. My grandfather moved here from Ireland and died in a riding accident in the north of England, where he'd met and married my grandmother. That's all there is to it. When she married Page's father and took the name of Masterton, she let her son take it too, as her first marriage had been so unhappy.' He made a wide gesture with his hands. 'There you have it.'

'So cut and dried,' she sneered. 'Like everything about you. Unfortunately, some people's lives aren't quite so uncomplicated as that.'

He grimaced. 'I'm sorry.'

But you aren't, Alex thought. She doubted if he'd ever done anything that he was sorry for in his life. She wasn't even sure if he was capable of experiencing real sympathy. They were two of a kind, he and Page.

'Are you saying yours has been complicated, Alex?'

She brought her lashes down like a dark veil over her emotions. 'Get lost,' she whispered, turning away.

'Don't want to talk to me?' He was, however, at the door before she was, those broad shoulders blocking out everything else. 'You know, you're behaving like a little schoolgirl. You look like one too, with that bear and that smudge on your face.' Before she could avoid it he had brought his thumb across the dark smear on her cheek. 'That's better.'

Was it? She could feel her pulses skittering out of control.

'You look pale,' he observed, studying her. 'Are you feeling all right?'

'I'm fine,' she lied, the effects of his casual touch with that suddenly solicitous regard undermining her defences.

'What's the matter?' he queried. 'Afraid I'm going to jump on you?' A wary emotion darkened her eyes and he laughed very quietly, as though he was laughing at himself. 'I thought you might like to see this.'

She frowned, only now realising that he was holding a book.

'I noticed you've nearly finished Byron,' he said, with a lift of his chin in the direction of the chair where she had been reading earlier.

Observant or observant! she thought as he handed it to her.

It was very old and dusty, but beautifully bound in black leather, a treasury of prose from one of England's most romantic poets, the letters on the cover embossed in gold.

Alex dropped the teddy down onto a chair. 'It's a first edition!' she breathed, opening the cover. 'Where did you find it?'

'In the loft.'

There was an inscription inside, too. 'To my love, Robert—Alexandra,' she read aloud. 'Who were they?' she asked, glancing up.

'You mean you don't know?'

She swallowed, meeting the censuring darkness of his eyes. Her throat felt dry, slightly sore. 'No, am I supposed to?'

Those eyes seemed to probe beyond the wary blue of hers to the hidden secrets beneath.

'My poor uninformed girl,' he drawled. 'My cousin really didn't tell you any of the things you ought to know, did she?'

Alex swallowed again. The dryness was still there. 'Like what?' she queried, reluctantly handing him back the book.

All he said, though, was, 'Hang onto it if you want to.'

'Can I?' Her throat might have felt funny, but her tone couldn't disguise the appreciation that was mirrored in her face. She wondered, though, why he was even trusting her with it—a rare and expensive heirloom—why he wasn't taunting her about her right even to be there, although he hadn't been—not so much anyway—over the past couple of days.

'Take it,' he said succinctly, before striding away.

The following morning when Alex woke up her throat felt as if she had swallowed a packet of razor-blades and her head felt as if it was splitting in two.

'I won't be needing any breakfast,' she croaked to Joyce Stern when she found the energy to lift the internal telephone. 'And don't bother about sending anyone up to clean the room today.' I'm going to die in it! she added silently with a painful grimace.

Fortunately, the housekeeper was diplomatic enough not to ask any questions. Consequently, Alex was surprised not only to hear a knock at her door several minutes later but to see York walk in in response to her feeble squawk.

'What on earth's happened to you?' In a dark pinstriped suit, he looked disgustingly healthy—in contrast to how she must appear, she thought, if her matted hair and hot cheeks and aching eyes were anything to go by!

'I've got bubonic plague,' she groaned. And there's a little man brandishing a sword around my tonsils! Unconsciously her fingers curled around her throat. 'So you'd better go away before it gets you too.'

He pulled a face, coming nearer. Why did he have to look so effortlessly dynamic?

'No problem. I've had it,' he said, palming her temple, then gently feeling both sides of her throat. His fingers were tender and cool. 'Your temperature's high and your glands are pretty swollen.'

And your hands smell of cologne, she thought, his touch sending sensations through her which she was much too weak not to succumb to this morning.

'I'm all right,' she said feebly. 'I don't need any looking after.'

'So you're going to get up and get your own meals, are you?' He looked amused, half-sceptical.

'I'm not hungry,' she croaked.

'No, but I'll bet you could certainly do with something to drink.'

Her throat craved something fruity, and her eyes were longing as they met his, though she was too proud actually to ask him to get something for her.

'I'll be back,' he told her, astute enough to guess.

He returned with a steaming mug of something.

'Freshly squeezed lemon, hot water, honey and...paracetamol,' he said in answer to her silent query, sitting down on the bed.

He held the tablet out for her to take. It was small and white against the dark strength of his hand.

'I've only got your word for that,' she quipped, sipping the liquid from the mug he had handed her. It was hot and lemony, unbelievably soothing as it slid down her burning throat.

'Take it,' he urged, suddenly impatient, and quickly she obeyed. 'We both know that if I wanted to render you powerless I wouldn't need any drug to do it for me.'

She kept her lashes lowered to hide her shaming disconcertion at the truth of his words. She had to be depraved to want him. Sick, she thought, popping the pill into her mouth.

It was still excruciating to swallow but the liquid was easing her throat by the second.

'Thanks,' she said when she had had enough, and as he took the mug from her she leaned back against the padded headboard, closing her eyes, murmuring almost unthinkingly, 'You're a godsend.'

'Really?' The amusement in his voice made her open them again. Even her lids were burning. 'I thought your opinion of me was that I was a devil.'

She didn't know what had made her say it but fleetingly, as her eyes locked with his, she felt a rush of something that sprang from more than just the powerful and indiscriminate chemistry. The strong lines of his face were etched with a hunger she hadn't recognised before— a dark, bleak hunger that crazily, for a moment, to her self-denigrating shame, made her want to reach out and touch the hard curve of his cheek, his jaw, that firm, resolute mouth...

'I want to go back to sleep,' she said with her eyelids drooping, shutting out her thoughts, because that was safer.

*   *   *

She was in bed for two days, by which time she was nursing a full-blown cold. A maid came several times to freshen the bathroom towels and see if she wanted anything. Even Joyce came up once or twice to ask if there was anything she could get her that would make her more comfortable, the concern beneath the well-scrubbed efficiency surprising Alex.

Funny how it took being ill, she thought, to see the better side of people. However, it was York's attentions that she found herself wanting and appreciating most—wanting even as her common sense would have rejected them.

'How do you feel?' he asked on that second afternoon, coming in and over to the bed, where she was sitting propped up by pillows.

Alex's pulse leapt to see him. He had been out since early that morning and, from his immaculate appearance, had obviously come fresh from some executive lunch.

'Don't ask,' she groaned. She didn't like his seeing her like this. Red-nosed. A blue satin wrap pulled around her over her matching nightie.

'Feeling any worse?' He moved a tray she had finished with from the bed and sat down. He smelt of fresh air and his own, disturbingly masculine scent.

'No, I want to get up,' she mumbled nasally, and promptly sneezed into the hanky she had at the ready.

A black eyebrow lifted in mocking disapproval. 'Not until tomorrow.'

'Who says so?'

'I do.'

And his word was law, she thought, feeling too rotten to argue against it—for the time being.

'It's all right for you,' she complained hoarsely. 'You ought to try lying here with no one to talk to and nothing to do. It's so *boring*.'

He made a wry gesture with his mouth. 'From the sound of that voice you shouldn't be talking.' He glanced over at the volume of poetry lying on the duvet on the far side of the bed. 'Have you finished the book?'

She shook her head, wincing as a dozen hammers seemed to strike up in unison inside it. 'I've read so much, I've given myself a headache.'

'Would you like a television brought up?'

She wrinkled her nose. 'There's enough soap in the bathroom,' she said drily.

'Oh, very droll.' He leaned forward, with his arms coming to rest on either side of her. 'A darned querulous little patient, aren't you?' he admonished softly.

She supposed she was, but she never was in the best of moods when she was ill, which fortunately was hardly ever.

'Well, what would you recommend that didn't overtax sore eyes and still manage to stimulate my intellect?' she enquired tremulously through the furore of emotions she felt just at his being there on her bed.

He said nothing, just got up, and she thought as he went out carrying the tray, Serves you right, you bad-tempered little fool. He despises you too much to put up with moodiness from you, for whatever reason. And some minutes afterwards, when her muffled senses caught the growl of his car starting up on the drive on the other side of the house, she felt even worse, her ears hanging onto the purr of the BMW's engine until it died away down the hill.

Come back, she pleaded silently, feeling lonely and depressed, until she realised and brought herself back to face common sense with a start.

What was she thinking? Wishing? She'd always hated the man. Disliked him as much as she disliked his hard-hearted uncle. They were both heartless, weren't they? So what was she doing letting York get under her skin like this?

Nevertheless, lying there, staring at the window so high above the garden that all she could see were trees tossed by a brisk March wind, she heard the first patter of raindrops on the glass, the mournful lowing of a cow on the adjoining farmland, and couldn't stop herself wishing he hadn't gone.

She was asleep when the door opened again, but woke up, expecting it to be dark, expecting it to be Joyce who had disturbed her, coming in with a hot drink.

But it wasn't dark and it wasn't the housekeeper.

'You,' she breathed with an illogical delight as her bleary eyes focused on York.

'Why so surprised?' He was carrying something under his arm. 'You wanted something a little more intel-lectual than soap.' Something rattled beneath the rustle of the brown paper bag he was opening. 'Something that wouldn't overtax your eyes. Will that do?' he said, tossing the green oblong box down onto the bed.

'Scrabble!' For the first time in two days a smile lit her eyes. So he'd gone out and bought it specially. And she'd thought...

'I see I've done something to satisfy you,' he drawled, tossing the screwed-up bag into the bin beside the dressing table.

Yes, he had, and it surprised her. Kindness from him was the last thing she'd expected.

'Why are you doing this?'

'Doing what?'

'Being nice to me,' she expanded, the paleness of her face allowing a closely guarded vulnerability to show through now as she met the dark inscrutability of his.

'What would you have me do?' he said rhetorically, moving away.

'Don't go.' It slipped out before she could help it.

There was a curious expression in his eyes as he turned around.

'Stay and play with me,' she suggested tentatively, feeling sheepish—perhaps even unwise—asking him.

'That's what they all say.' His wry remark made her colour rise, wish she'd been more careful in her choice

of words. 'Are you sure you want me to?' It was a soft,
subtle reminder of the gulf that lay between them.

Fortunately, though, at that moment she felt a sneeze
coming on and grabbed her hanky, so that she didn't
need to answer, and when she looked up again he had
tossed his jacket down at the foot of the bed and was
loosening his tie, coming over to pick up the phone.

'Send up some coffee, will you, Joyce? And a glass
of something for the invalid. Thanks.'

Even before the receiver had clicked back onto its rest,
Alex felt a warm glow spreading through her body.

You aren't well. That's all this is, she told herself cau-
tioningly. You're just desperate for company, and he's
the only one around.

Desperate, however, though she might have been, she
was startled to realise, as the afternoon slid into evening
and York switched on the light, that there wasn't really
anyone else whom she wanted to be with, that she was
actually enjoying being with York. Perhaps it was because she was ill, but that usual, unrelenting hostility
towards her had been absent over the past couple of days,
and today he seemed positively approachable. Nor did
she feel her usual need to be on the defensive with him,
so that the time passed in a strangely guarded affinity.

Ron telephoned him once during the afternoon to
discuss some problem at the quarry. One of his directors
in the London office rang too and, listening to him as
he gave orders and advice, suggested solutions for multimillion-pound problems over the phone, Alex realised
how valuable his time was, marvelling at that keen brain
that enabled him to converse on one vital and important
level and still manage to play a trivial yet winning game
of Scrabble with her!

'I promised the customer next week and I expect it to
be finalised by then.' His voice held indisputable authority. He was accepting no excuses for laxity.

Alex put an obscure word on the board. She wasn't sure if she had spelt it correctly. She sent a glance up at York who was still talking, saw him shaking his head. Her eyes widened in amazement, an emotion his acknowledged with wry amusement.

How could he even be half-aware of what she was doing as well? she marvelled further, following the rules of the game and removing her letters, wondering how he managed to keep that private amusement from his director, although he did. Running an empire was child's play to him, she decided. Like playing Monopoly—or Scrabble!

He was leaning back on his chair now, clasping one dark-trousered leg across his knee. His shirt was unbuttoned at the throat. She could see his flesh, a dark contrast against the pure white cotton. And where his trouser leg had ridden up she could see his bare leg above the black sock. Bronze, furred with dark hair...

'Do you want to go on with this? Or are we playing strip poker now?'

She hadn't realised he had come off the phone, too absorbed in her studied appreciation of him to notice, and embarrassed colour made her cheeks almost as red as her sore nose.

'That's wishful thinking, isn't it?' She endeavoured to sound half-indignant, but York merely laughed.

'On whose part?'

Not on mine! she wanted to toss back, but hesitated too long. Anyway, it wouldn't have been true. Shamefully, the sexuality she had tried to deny, to repress in herself for so long made her secretly confess now that she would love to undress him, to feel the warmth of his skin beneath her fingers, the muscles flexing, bunching as she caressed him, like velvet hardening to steel...

'Wait until you're better, Alex.' His voice was softly mocking, as though he had just read her outrageous thoughts. 'And keep your mind on your game—unless, of course... you want me to beat you.'

How could she keep her mind on it? He looked so excitingly male, his eyes dark with sensual teasing, that unconsciously she touched her top lip with her tongue.

'You'll beat me anyway,' she breathed, light-headed from the sensations that raced uncontrollably through her.

'Do you always agree to surrender so readily?' The hard angles of his face were softened by that teasing innuendo.

'Your turn.' She could hardly get it out, her voice cracking from what she hoped he would think was her cold. 'I had to take my letters off, remember?'

'Ah, yes.' Despite this sensual repartee with her, he was still in control of the game, looking smug and darkly intent as his eyes scanned the scoreboard. 'Well, would you believe it! I can get a triple word score, plus all my letters out—which would make another fifty points for using all seven at once—if I can just substitute this J for an O...'

'Hey, that's cheating!' Unbelievably, he had dropped the redundant J back into the lid of the box and was turning over the remaining little cream squares that had been lying face down, looking for his O.

'Do we ever get anywhere if we don't cheat a little sometimes? Anyway, I prefer to call it bending the rules... Got it!' he laughed.

Face triumphant, he was about to add the substituted letter to the little wooden rack that contained his six other letters but, protesting, Alex grabbed at his wrist.

'That's not fair! I thought this was a serious game.'

'So what are you going to do?' Laughter lines crinkled around his eyes. 'Fight me for it?'

She followed the path of his gaze to her fingers clasped around his wrist, feeling the corded strength of his

tendons, the slow, steady rhythm of his pulse beneath
the bronze skin.

'No, I...' Flushing, she shrank back, dropping his wrist
as if it were a lethal object, regretting her impulsive
action. He laughed very softly, his eyes holding hers,
and she knew they were assessing her trembling agi-
tation, but she couldn't look away. Thankfully the phone
rang then. His eyes still on her, he hesitated, as though
disinclined to answer it. Then he picked it up.

'Hello, Kay.' If her touching him had affected him in
any way at all, he didn't show it. 'No, nothing important,' he said, and she wondered if he was referring
to what he had been doing before the woman rang.

Trying not to eavesdrop, not to show that she was the
slightest bit interested in anything he might have to say
to his girlfriend, she picked up the poetry book that was
still lying on the bed.

'To my love, Robert—Alexandra.' Distractedly, her
eyes scanned the inscription on the flyleaf. He had said
she was supposed to know who they were, only she
didn't. To my love, Kay—York. The words seemed to
jolt through her brain as mentally she substituted them
for the originals. Well, wasn't that what they were doing?
Substituting letters? What did it matter if he did love
Kay Weatherby? He probably did. Why should she care?
She didn't belong here, wasn't part of this family. She
never had been.

Why, then, did she suddenly feel so dispirited as he
came off the phone? Was it because that firm, masculine mouth was curved in an absent smile, as though
Kay had said something to make him happy? So what
if she had?

'OK.' He leaned to the task in hand, using the unethi-
cally acquired O to join up with the R of her BEAR—a
simple word she had put down in desperation because
her brain had been too fogged to think of anything else.
But now, as he finished laying out the last of his little

cream tiles, his word seemed to leap out at her, emblazoned as it was across the board.

IMPOSTOR

Her gaze, direct and challenging, clashed with his, hooded and unfathomable.

'It's spelt with an E,' she said, swallowing.

'It can be either,' he said softly, confidently. 'But I believe the dictionary favours O.'

So why had he felt the need to put it down? To gauge her reaction? Had she still not managed to convince him? she thought, almost past caring now.

'It's a good word,' she commended, refusing to rise to his bait and start defending herself against his silent yet blatant accusation. 'A pity you had to stoop to such unethical means to get it.'

'It's called making the most of one's opportunities.' He smiled, getting up. 'Something I think you know a little about too, don't you...cousin?' He stooped to kiss her lightly on the forehead. 'I have to go now, but thanks for the game. We'll have to do it again some time.'

And he was gone, leaving Alex feeling frustrated and abandoned: frustrated because she felt she was playing a losing game with him in more than just the obvious, abandoned because she had the strongest suspicion that he had gone to meet Kay.

CHAPTER SIX

ALEX felt considerably better the next day and was able to get up. And the day after that, feeling restless, she was surprised when York suggested she might like to help Joyce, who was sorting through the cupboards in what had been his uncle's bedroom.

'You trust me that far?'

She couldn't contain the little jibe as he swung away from the breakfast table, preparing to leave for the day, but he merely shrugged and said, 'I'm sure you can't do much harm under Joyce's supervision. And as I've got to put up with you temporarily you may as well earn your keep.'

'Thanks,' she responded tartly, although she wondered if she had imagined that almost amused note in his voice as he'd turned away.

That first day, turning out items into two piles—one for the refuse sack, the other for York's attention—she formed a remarkable camaraderie with the housekeeper as they ploughed through their task. Then the next day Joyce went shopping, leaving Alex to carry on alone. Obviously having fewer misgivings about her than York did! she thought drily, wondering what he'd say if he knew. And it was that afternoon, while turning out the last items in one of the cupboards, that she found the letters.

They were in a bundle, tied with an old ribbon, lying on the floor as though they had long ago slipped off the back of a shelf and been forgotten, but as soon as she realised what they were, swiftly Alex took them back to her room.

Her heart was beating fast, her fingers trembling as she locked her door. Subsiding onto the bed, she untied the faded ribbon, feeling like a criminal as she unfolded the first letter, started to read.

It was what she had been looking for for days, been hoping—praying—that she would find. It was what Lonnie Burrowes would have called 'a scoop', she recognised as she sat there, reliving the love and the passion between a young Shirley Masterton and her equally young lover. But there was more. Oh, so much more!

If Lonnie got his hands on this, he would have a field-day! she realised distractedly. Lonnie and others like him. The papers they represented would be willing to pay a fortune for the agonies of a family as newsworthy as this!

Numbly, she got to her feet, only to sink down again on a chair, tortured by so many emotions that it was difficult to separate one from the other.

Ever since she had come here she had been searching for these letters—sometimes, she'd thought, in vain; she'd thought that she'd be going home empty-handed, with nothing but the scars of York's raw contempt and suspicion to remind her of a wasted trip. And now...

She sat there for a long time, wrestling with the sadness and guilt and anger that were bubbling to the surface inside her. Anger at herself. At Page. At Shirley. Perhaps it was more than a little understandable, if York knew the truth, why he found it so difficult to forgive.

Yes, Lonnie would love to get his hands on this, she reflected bitterly, but it was *her* story. Her own personal exclusive.

The words tasted like poison on her tongue as she remembered the fleeting desire that day in the churchyard to drag York down from his high horse. Only it wasn't York who was taking the fall...

It was a long time later that she eventually dragged herself across the room to the telephone, forced her cold, stiff fingers to tap out the number from the little card she had taken from her purse.

*   *   *

She wasn't even aware of a car pulling up, nor of the driver's door closing. Lost in her own thoughts, Alex didn't even notice York's almost silent approach along the tree-lined path until he spoke her name.

'Alexia.'

Without turning round, startled, Alex sucked in her breath. It was the first time he had called her that since that bitter March day he had seen her standing here, next to his uncle's grave.

Panic, though, rushed through her. He couldn't see her like this!

'Go away,' she ordered in a tight, muffled voice.

'Alexia—look at me.'

Whether she would have answered that imperative note in his voice, she didn't know, because he didn't give her the chance to find out. Strong fingers on her arm were pulling her round, exposing her to him. Her face was red and blotchy and she recognised something like sympathy in his as he saw the tears cascading down her cheeks.

'He loved my mother,' she sobbed, not caring any more about pride or dignity or how vulnerable she might appear to him. 'Page. I hated him for what he did, but he loved her. He wrote to her, asking for her forgiveness—begging her to come home—but she sent his letter back.'

It had been there, tied in that bundle with all the others, the envelope marked clearly in her mother's familiar handwriting, 'Return to Sender'.

'What did you imagine?' York's tone was gently chiding. 'She *was* his only child.'

For a moment his gaze moved past her, down to the single red rose she had placed on the newly laid chippings, and as though he had broken some spell with that small action she said, puzzled, 'How did you know where to find me?'

'The card with the taxi firm on it. You left it on the bedside cabinet. I rang them and asked where they'd taken you.'

She looked up at him, frowning. 'Did you know about the letters?'

'Between your mother and father?' He nodded.

'They really loved each other.' She sniffed.

'Yes.'

'Did you read them?' she queried, searching those dark, inscrutable features.

He shook his head. 'I didn't think it was my place to. Page told me about them a long time ago. He'd found them beneath a loose floorboard.'

'I know. My mother hid them. She told me about them and I wanted them as a keepsake—of both my parents. Despite what you've thought, it was the only reason I stayed when I heard my grandfather had died. I know you'll never believe it, but I did want to see him again— I just got your letter too late, that was all—but that was my main reason for coming. With him gone, those letters seemed like the only thing left to remind me of my roots, where I came from. I didn't want you finding them . . . throwing them out.' A small note of rebellion broke through her sobs. 'When I couldn't find them I thought you'd already done it.'

'Why didn't you ask me?' he probed.

Why? Because he'd seemed so hard-hearted that she'd thought he'd probably laugh in her face at her foolish sentimentality. Now, though, she wasn't sure . . .

'He regretted splitting them up, stopping them from marrying, and he wanted Shirley to know how sorry he was.' She sniffed again, deciding not to answer his last question. Her expression as she tilted her head was tortured, filled with her own regret. 'Why do you think he put that letter with the others? In the hope that someone—that perhaps *I* might find it?' she queried sadly.

York's mouth was a tight, tense line. 'I don't know,' he said. 'I only know it was just a few days after Shirley returned it that he had his first stroke.'

His tone assured her that he held his cousin solely responsible. His hatred for Shirley burned as strongly as ever, making Alex wince. She had been her mother, after all. 'I never knew,' she uttered, forcing back a sob.

'How could you?' The wind in the trees seemed to emulate the sigh that lifted from his chest. 'After Shirley died and I came to see you, you were so full of hatred and bitterness you wouldn't have listened even if I'd tried to explain.'

No, I wouldn't have, she thought, remembering the starkness of his face when he'd come to see her in that crummy little flat she'd shared with her mother. She realised now he must have been suffering deep personal anguish. She'd just thought him cold and cruel in his demands for her to return home. She'd been just eighteen at the time and, as he'd said, so bitter about the way Shirley had suffered through her father's interference in her life that she had been blind to anything he might have been feeling, so that all she had wanted was to lash out at the one strong connection with Page Masterton.

'If he wants me back so much—why didn't he come himself?' were the words she had thrown at him out of her own poignant grief and unhappiness. 'But no, he couldn't! He sent you, didn't he? The man who always gets results!'

Only, she hadn't gone. And then, afraid of him—of her shaming and illogical attraction to him and the hard surveillance she knew he was keeping on her—she had taken off within weeks. She'd left the country and, so that she couldn't be found, taken a derivative of her father's name with the short form of her own that she had always hated; York had been right about that. But he *had* found her, in spite of it, she thought with a little shiver, eventually—even though, when she'd got his letter, it had been too late.

'I would have persisted had it been left to me,' he said, breaking in on her tumultuous thoughts. 'I would never have let you go away and lose touch with him as you did. But when he realised you didn't want anything to do with him he told me to let it go.'

'And of course you did everything he asked.' It was an accusation, but directed more at herself, more at her own naïvety and blindness than anything else.

'No,' he said. 'I kept tabs on you for a while—before you disappeared. I went to America for several weeks— on business—and when I came back and checked on you again—you'd gone. I never dreamt for one moment that you'd emigrated. I thought you'd gone abroad, perhaps, but not as far as New Zealand. You seemed too young— much too vulnerable...'

'But I grew up, York,' she assured him bitterly. 'And fast.'

'I suppose you had to.' That sagacious note in his voice surprised her. Had he guessed how hard it had been to be a naïve female adolescent entirely alone in a strange country, a strange continent? 'It shouldn't have been necessary, though.' And with unmistakable admonition he said, 'You should have come back where you belonged. Maybe I should have been much more insistent. I don't know. But then you always were ready to rebel against me, weren't you, Alexia? Never knew quite how to deal with that contrary mixture of hatred and attraction you felt for what was, after all, your mother's cousin.'

'No!' she denied hotly, but they both knew better.

He laughed then, ever so quietly, surprising her again as he pulled her gently against him.

Sensations assailed her as for one moment she thought he was going to kiss her. Instead, though, he held her to him, as if he were cradling a child, and, as if it were the most natural thing to do, she wound her arms around the hard circumference of his waist inside his jacket, her head against his chest, revelling in his warmth, in those strong, caressing fingers lost in her hair.

Oh, to be held so tenderly by him! Without any animosity. Without feeling that need in him to punish and dominate her through her own weak desire.

'Does this mean you believe me now?' she breathed censoriously into the expensive silk of his shirt. He smelt wonderful. Subtly exotic. Extremely male. 'Did it have to take seeing me so...sick with contrition—?'

'No.' His response was firm, without hesitation. 'I've known for some time.'

'Like when?' Surprised, her face was upturned to the dark underside of his jaw shaded by nearly a day's growth of stubble.

'Oh, things you said. The poetry. Your passion for it. Page shared the same passion. After his last stroke it was all he did day and night—read poetry like it was going out of fashion. Those lines you quoted when we were at Lorna Doone Valley that day—it was from his favourite.' Which was why he'd nearly put them both into the hedge at the time, she reflected, equally amazed. 'And if I'd still been in any doubt—which I wasn't— Mother sent me a photograph of Page's mother, your great-grandmother, Alexandra. The one you were named after.'

'The one whose inscription is in that book you let me borrow,' Alex realised aloud.

'Let you *keep*. It's yours more than mine,' he surprised her by saying, but, of course, she was a direct descendant, while he... 'It seems her name wasn't the only thing she passed on to you,' he went on to inform her intriguingly. 'She couldn't have been in any more than her late twenties when the photograph was taken but she was every bit as silver as you are.'

'Really?' She was smiling, fascinated. Then, as it dawned on her, she demanded, 'So why didn't you tell me?' She exhaled indignantly, drawing back from him.

'Perhaps because you were the one who kept it up—always implying that I thought you were an impostor. And maybe—' he caught her arms, preventing her from pulling away '—just a little—because I liked seeing you frustrated,' he confessed, with no lack of dignity in his admission. 'I thought you were just after the inheritance and so I felt you deserved to be frustrated after the way Page had suffered.'

Of course, he had cared deeply about Page; she had recognised that from the beginning. But he had no such feeling for her.

'Bastard,' she breathed, wondering why she suddenly felt so deflated.

'Maybe,' he acknowledged, and smiled because, of course, he knew that even in spite of that she had been powerless to resist him, that she still was, which was probably why he dipped his head then and kissed her remarkably gently on the mouth, to prove it to himself, and her—an action that brought her hands up involuntarily under his jacket, exploring the firm muscles of his back, clutching him to her as their mouths became more urgent, seeking, fervent with a hunger that neither could contain.

He was her only family—all she had in the world—and in that capacity she wanted his love, she realised now. But she wanted more from him. Much more than that. This wasn't a familial feeling, this need to be close to him. This was something deeper, much more encompassing...

Suddenly, though, he was breaking the kiss.

'It wasn't the place before,' he reminded her gently with a smile in his voice, 'and it most definitely isn't the place now. I think we'd better leave before we bring the vicar's wrath down on our heads.'

He stood away from her and, without looking up, Alex stepped nimbly past him, her emotions a confusion of exhilaration and despair. That she was in danger of falling in love with him was obvious. But that she could ever expect him to feel the same way about her...

'No, don't...' She put up her hands to hold him off when he reached for her in the car just outside the gates. Things were happening too fast, getting beyond her control.

'Why not?' he pressed quietly. 'Do you still think I'm the big, bad ogre who wanted you and your mother out of the way so I could wheedle my way into Page's affections—and his pocket—make myself number-one heir? Or are you blaming me for backing up your grandfather in wanting to see that you were brought up decently, that you didn't turn into the sort of little tramp you clearly seemed destined to become? Because, seventeen though you were, you certainly didn't have any qualms about trying to seduce a man. Or perhaps you've pledged a lifelong vendetta against me for not taking you to bed that night, is that it? Hell hath no fury et cetera. Because, if I had been any other man, I probably would have.'

Alex flinched from the memory of that night, the last time she had been at Moorlands. It had haunted her for ten years, the shame torturing her, the sensuality he had awakened in her so profound that she had known months of feverish, disturbing dreams, the conviction that she was somehow profane contributing to her refusal ever to allow herself even to come close to feeling the same degree of desire for any man since.

'It—it wasn't like that.' She had to convince him. Otherwise he would always believe the worst about her, think that she was loose, anybody's, as he had accused her of being that day he'd seen Lonnie leaving. Like... She closed her eyes against a lacerating anguish, heard him put the key in the ignition although he didn't start the engine. God, he couldn't think that. 'I had no intention of seducing you. That wasn't why I was in your room.'

'Tell me about it,' he invited, the leather squeaking beneath him as he sat back, his face hard and intent, giving her no quarter.

She didn't even want to remember, let alone talk about it, but the memory surged back, forcing her to relive, in shamingly graphic detail, the events of that last night ten years ago.

She hadn't known then why her mother had brought her to Moorlands. Perhaps it had been an attempt at reconciliation with her family. Perhaps she'd never know. But during their brief visit Page had arranged a trip abroad—ostensibly for them all—and, intimidated though she had been by her autocratic grandfather and his forceful, formidable nephew, Alex had been looking forward to it. That had been until the night her mother had come up to her room to inform her that the trip planned for the following day didn't include her, Shirley.

'Your grandfather's already in London and he's instructed York to drive you up there tomorrow—on your own,' the woman had told her feverishly. She could still see Shirley's lovely, agitated face, her flushed cheeks and desperate brown eyes. The bright auburn hair. 'Their plan's to get you as far away from me as they possibly can—to split us up, Alexia. But York's out at the moment and he hasn't taken the car. If you could sneak into his room and see if you can find the keys, we could get away tonight—without anyone knowing. I'll drive us as far as the station. Then when we're far enough away I can ring and tell him where we've left the car.'

Even now the thought of what Shirley had expected of her could still send tremors down her spine. Entering York's room, even when he wasn't in it, had been, for her, as daunting as walking into a lion's cage. She had found him terrifyingly attractive even then.

'Why do I have to do it? Why can't you?' she remembered asking.

And Shirley's reply. 'I know this house like the back of my hand. What excuse could I give if someone saw me? But if anyone sees you you can at least pretend you've wandered into the wrong room. If you won't do it, the chances are we'll be separated for good—just like I was from your father. We may never see each other again. Is that what you want?'

Sitting at the dressing table where she had been experimenting with make-up, Alex had stared petulantly at her less than familiar reflection. 'He can't make me go anywhere I don't want to!' she'd declared in such naïve defiance of York that it was laughable now. So was the way she must have looked—the glasses she hated discarded, eyelids heavy with shadow, just a little too much lipstick, and her long black hair backcombed into a wild, enticing frenzy of curls.

'Your grandfather's influential enough—he can make you do anything.' Shirley's warning attempted to curb her rising rebellion. 'As for York, you'll be in for a rude awakening, my girl, if you think he'll stand for any sort of revolt from a slip of a kid like you.'

Alarmed more by how York rather than her grandfather might deal with her if she refused to go with him, she did as Shirley asked.

The room was darker than she'd expected, as the curtains were already drawn, but enough light spilled onto the practical chest of drawers across the room for her to see his car keys on top.

Quickly she went to pick them up, but before her fingers could close around them something stirred in the bed—the long, powerfully built limbs of the man whom she both feared and nursed a violent attraction for.

'Alexia?' He sat up, squinting almost painfully from the light from the door, as though he'd had a headache, his hair tousled, his chest bare, the sudden lithe movement with which he sprang out of bed causing her to press herself back against the chest of drawers. 'What are you doing here?'

He was already reaching for a robe while she wrestled with the nervous excitement of seeing him naked—naked except for a pair of dark underpants—the perfect masculinity of that darkly haired chest and tight waist down to the hard musculature of his long legs making her forget to use the feeble excuse she'd believed she had had prepared as she uttered shakily, 'I—I...don't know. I...wanted to see you.'

'Oh?' He came towards her, fastening his robe, that amused twist on his lips unable to hide wholly his bafflement, as frantically Alex wondered how she was going to get away from him.

In only her flimsy nightdress, with her face made up to the nines, it was no wonder, she thought now, that he'd thought her the promiscuous little tramp he'd accused her of being!

'Why? Why did you want to see me?'

Of course she hadn't been able to answer. There was nothing she could have said that could have backed up that unthinking little utterance at her shock at finding him there!

She had felt his thumb running over the smudges of the lipstick she'd been trying on before Shirley had come to her with her request, and she had been able only to look up at him, speechless, with huge, hungry eyes, the heavy lifting of her breasts that had come from her heart's pounding fear of him making her look like the excited little siren he thought wanted him to take her to bed.

'Is it for this?'

Nothing could have prepared her for the masterful way in which his mouth covered hers, for that surge of sensation as his arms went around her far too curvy yet untutored body. She knew a gushing in her ears, like drowning, and clung to him to stop her knees buckling under her from the dizzying excitement he was generating in her.

When he let her go, like the young fool she was, all she could do was stare up at him and say breathlessly, 'You—you love me?'

Even now she shivered as she remembered his harsh laugh, the way his mouth had become hard with blatant disdain.

'*Love* you? What sort of man do you think you're playing with, Alexia?'

'I...' His anger had been frightening. How could he kiss her like that and then turn so savage? she'd wondered in her foolish naïvety. She'd felt faint, her mouth dry, and lamely she'd murmured, 'I—I need a drink of water.'

His hands had gripped painfully on her upper arms.

'I know what you need, young lady, and it isn't water! I think a damn good hiding would be more beneficial to you, before you're any further along the promiscuous little path you're clearly headed down!'

Whether he would have carried out his threat, she never found out, because it was at that moment that Shirley, probably realising how long she was taking, chose to come in.

'What on earth...?' Shirley stood transfixed by the door. 'York?' She looked questioningly from her daughter to York and back to Alexia again, still trembling in his grasp. 'Alexia?' There was hard suspicion on her beautiful face. 'What—what the hell's going on?'

Shamed by her uncontrolled response to York's kiss and the brutal rejection that followed, Alex couldn't utter a word. But *he* did. Harshly and coldly, without any attempt to lessen her shame.

'Perhaps it's about time you realised exactly what's happening to your daughter, Shirley. That she's already well on the way to becoming an inveterate little vamp. Now can you see why Page has had his worries about her upbringing? What she needs is someone to show her a better example of morality before someone less scrupulous than I am decides to take her to bed!'

Shirley's lips twisted in anger, but it was Alex who took the initial brunt of what she later realised was jealousy. 'Is that why you put all that muck on your face?' Shirley accused her, pulling her round. 'Is that what you were hoping?'

Alex's feeble, 'No! I didn't want to come in here, remember?' induced the hard suspicion that suddenly burned on York's face.

'What is this? Some little scheme concocted between the two of you to compromise me?' he snarled, that frighteningly masculine anger taking some of the wind out of Shirley's sails.

'Of course not.' Shirley pushed her aside. 'York, would we do that?' Her mother's voice softened in disputable allure. 'I have to get away from your uncle, York. You know he hates me. But you—you could come with us. Take Alex in hand. She needs a man's control. And I...' Sickened, she watched Shirley's trembling hands slide persuasively over the bronze chest which, only moments before, had been crushing her own young breasts. 'I could be good for you. Please, York. We could be good together. I've always thought so. I'd do anything for you. All you'd have to do is ask. Please...'

'Thanks—but no thanks.' Roughly he dragged down the hands that had crept around his neck. 'I prefer my women with at least some ethics—'

His sentence was splintered as Shirley's hand struck a hard blow across his face, then another and another.

Hopelessly, Alex watched as her mother entirely lost control, unable to take the same shaming rejection her daughter had just taken, until York, his hair falling untidily across his forehead, was left with little option but to take hold of her and forcibly shake her.

When he let her go she almost fell backwards. That was when she took hold of Alex and pushed her violently out of the room. And though they had left that night, as Shirley had wanted to, taking that cold, miserable bus ride to the station, Alex remembered now that things had never been quite the same between them after that. Shirley had started staying out late, drinking more, mixing with dubious company—until that afternoon when she, Alex, happy and unsuspecting, had come home from secretarial college unexpectedly early because her exams were over...

She shut her mind against the shock and pain stirring cruelly inside of her.

Almost a year after leaving Moorlands her mother had been dead, leaving her to fend for herself, bitter and alone.

'It wasn't my uncle's intention to split you up,' York stated quietly when she'd finished telling him her version of the facts. 'He'd planned that trip hoping it would help to patch things up with your mother, but as usual they had a row and she refused to go or to let you go with him. He'd asked me to bring you anyway as he knew how much you'd been looking forward to it. I think he hoped Shirley would see sense and join us, but obviously he hadn't realised what a bitterly unforgiving creature his daughter was.'

His unrelenting hatred of her mother cut deeply into Alex. She wanted to say something in the woman's defence, but the words wouldn't come.

'She must have had her reasons—for refusing to come back—or even acknowledging his letter,' she said sadly at length, considering that envelope marked 'Return to Sender'. 'After all, you've thought badly of me all these years...'

'Yes.' That simple syllable was redolent with meaning and she glanced quickly away as his gaze caught hers, knowing what he was thinking. 'If you were sent to my room on an errand—had no intention of finding me there,' he said, sitting forward with one dark-sleeved arm across the steering wheel, 'why were you so responsive when I kissed you?'

'I don't know.'

'Why are you now?'

'I don't know!'

'Even though you profess to despise me.'

'I don't *know*!'

'And with just cause, from your version of events.' Mercilessly, he caught her shoulders, forcing her to meet the probing intensity of his gaze. 'Why, Alexia?'

She didn't answer, lowering her lashes so that her gaze was resting on the subtle blue knot of his tie.

'I'll tell you why,' he said decisively. 'There's something between us that time, distance and even animosity can't extinguish. You feel it every time I look at you. I know—I'm not blind. And I—' He exhaled heavily, as though in long-suffering remorse. 'You were little more than a child, yet I don't know how I stopped myself from making love to you that night. A wild Lolita. So tempting and at the same time so innocent...'

It was building between them now, that almost irrepressible urge for each to reach for the other, to lose themselves in a passion that would be as fierce as it was uncontrolled. She could hear it in the hoarse quality of his voice, feel it in the throbbing tension in her loins, which she knew would only ever be sated by nights of endless ecstasy in his bed. But, taking another deep breath, all he said as he started the engine was, 'Let's go home.'

CHAPTER SEVEN

OVER the next two or three weeks, Alex felt her relationship with York improving considerably. Together they sorted through the rest of the house, exchanged opinions and ideas for freshening up the decor—a coat of paint here, some revarnishing there. Workmen were called in and the agreed repairs and changes were begun.

'What are you going to do, sell it?' she asked one morning, when she was helping him take down curtain tracks above the dining room's high leaded windows. It seemed a pity to think of Moorlands in anyone else's hands.

'I'll never sell it,' was all he said from the top of the stepladder, and with such firm resolve that she wondered if it sprang from resentment at not having complete dominion over its future. After all, he had to consult her on every decision taken about it, didn't he?

'Supposing I want to buy your share?' she suggested, although she had never considered even half the house hers, let alone ever owning it all!

'Could you?' He stepped lithely down off the steps onto the dustsheet, taking the tracking she'd been holding steady for him before reaching for the mug of freshly brewed coffee she had brought in earlier. She didn't have to answer. He knew she couldn't buy it. Even if she chose to use the allowance Page had so generously left her, she knew she would never be able to secure a mortgage on a place like Moorlands.

'Would you accept a two-hundred-year repayment plan?' she joked instead, her blue eyes twinkling, secretly feasting on the hard, lean power of him beneath the white T-shirt and jeans as he moved to set his mug down on the steps.

'No, if I was selling it to you—which I'm not,' he stated decisively, 'you could stay here and pay me in kind.'

She blushed at that and said, deliberately misinterpreting his remark, 'You mean as chief cook and bottle-washer?'

He looked up from the task of unscrewing a bracket on the tracking that was resting on his knee. 'That wasn't what I meant and you know it.'

Alex swallowed. No, he meant as his siren, his dutiful little sex-slave—because she would be dutiful in that, wallowing in her own capitulation to him, unable to help herself. Although, even knowing that, he hadn't actually crossed the barrier to make himself her lover. She could only assume that he was treading cautiously with her as he had been since that day he had found her crying in the churchyard.

She was his cousin, nothing more, and while he probably no longer felt the need to punish her, having witnessed her abject remorse over Page, he didn't want any complications with regard to Moorlands either—though sometimes he couldn't resist reminding her of that lethal chemistry that was always there between them, influencing everything they said and did.

'You can fill the house with as many women as you want—after I've gone,' she said, trying to sound nonchalant, because the thought of leaving him and returning to New Zealand was causing her deeper anguish by the day.

With her grandfather dead, and since she had found those letters, she had no further reason to stay, and she had accepted York's invitation to do so only out of courtesy to Page's memory, as well as to help York with the vast amount of work that needed doing, sorting through and clearing out his uncle's personal effects.

And though she hadn't been as close to her grandfather as she would now dearly love to have been—while York had been as close to him as a son—there was, nonetheless, a blood tie between her and the late Page Masterton that nothing could sever. She felt she owed him something. Besides, her job with the television studio was on a freelance basis anyway, and she had already given them notice of indefinite absence. 'I'm sure you could find dozens of drooling fans,' she added more pointedly than she intended, 'willing to share this place with you.'

'True.' His conceit was intentional, she decided, and knew he could sense her contentious gaze burning on the shining ebony of his bowed head. 'But supposing I only want one?' He looked up then, one smouldering glance over her well-filled T-shirt and slender, denim-covered hips causing her stomach to turn a somersault, so that she laughed like some nervous schoolgirl.

'I'm sure Kay Weatherby will make a wonderful mistress,' she uttered, desperate to know how he felt about the woman and unable to help thinking, as she sent an agitated glance round the elegant room, that Kay would probably look very much at home running this beautiful house.

'No,' he countered sombrely then. 'Kay will make some man a very proper and presentable wife. But not me, I'm afraid. She's much too clinging and possessive. And why would I want any other woman around when I've got you to wait on me and cater to all my creature comforts?'

'You...!' Her relief in realising that he wasn't serious about Kay superseded by outrage at that last remark, she showed him just what she thought of his supreme arrogance by making him drop the tracking to deflect the full impact of the heavy valance she had been folding and now flung at him. 'Chauvinist!'

'Temper, temper!' he laughed, catching the dark green velvet somewhere around waist level. 'That's one thing I'm learning about you—along with your incapacity to bounce out of bed bright and breezy in the mornings.'

So he'd noticed that!

'I can't help it if I can't make civil conversation before eight o'clock!' she threw back, in amiable defence of her inability to start each day in dynamo mode as he seemed to be able to. 'No one should be expected to.'

'Oh, I'm not complaining.' He grinned. 'In fact it's rather engaging.'

'Why?' Her head was tilted in mock challenge. She was getting used to his teasing now. 'Because you don't know I'm here?' she suggested, and with assumed indignation flounced away from him, her hands stuffed into the pockets of her jeans.

'Oh, I'm very aware that you're here, Alexia.' The teasing in his voice had become wholly sensual and, taken off guard, she gasped as the velvet valance was suddenly thrown around her so that he could drag her back into the unrelenting circle of his arms. 'I'm very much aware that you're here. As for the temper, it just shows that you haven't lost that spirited, passionate nature.'

'You've got one too,' she reminded him, her throat clogging, her hands pressing in futile defence against the warm, solid wall of his chest. The faint scent of his perspiration was arousing. Incredibly erotic... 'Worse than mine.'

'In that case someone will need to stand by with a fire extinguisher if ever we find ourselves in bed together.'

She could feel his heart beneath that powerful ribcage, thundering in unison with her own. His face was a complexity of smouldering emotions and when he dipped his head she closed her eyes, waiting for a kiss that didn't come.

'Getting involved with one's cousin, I've decided, isn't something I would necessarily advocate,' he murmured deeply, his face mere inches from hers.

Of course. She wasn't someone he could just have an affair with and toss aside when he grew tired of her. She was related to him—albeit only by marriage. There were rules to observe.

'Who says I want to get involved with you?' she contended, her fingers trembling against the soft cotton of his T-shirt.

His gaze took in the bright blue eyes with their dilated pupils, the trembling of her soft mouth, and he offered a rather wan smile. 'You are involved,' he said quietly.

Of course she was—desperately! she realised, seeing in the intensity of his magnificent features a hunger every bit as strong as hers—a dark and compelling need of her that was all the more powerful for its suppression, calling on every last atom of his restraint.

Her lashes fluttered closed; she couldn't meet his gaze. Her voice was a tremor as she murmured, recognising the truth in what she said, 'So are you.'

His body tensed. She could feel it in the hardening muscle. For one terrifying and glorious moment she thought he was going to give into the desires that threatened his self-control, plunge them both into an unwise and complicated situation from which there could be no turning back.

Then one of the painters called to him from the doorway. She caught York's shuddering sigh before he let the valance fall, releasing her, leaving her mourning his arms, and though she knew she should have been glad that nothing had happened she couldn't contain that ache of reckless longing that sprang not only from the physical desires he aroused in her but as much, if not more, from being in love with him.

Because she was in love with him. She couldn't deny that even if she wanted to now. And maybe he knew it, which was perhaps why, she surmised as April slid into May and then that month also slipped by, he continued to treat her with, only at best, light-hearted teasing and, at worst, tolerant indifference.

She knew she had surprised him with her knowledge of and thirst for poetry—which she had been happy to realise she had inherited from Page—just as she knew she had surprised him with her enthusiastic interest in his work. And he was knowledgeable in every field, it seemed, able to converse with her on any subject, on any level.

Once, taking her on a drive to a small harbour town further up the coast, he had her laughing with a dramatic recital of *The Ancient Mariner*, surprising her with the information that Coleridge had been inspired to write his famous poem probably on the very stroll that they were taking.

'Would he have had his BMW parked in the same place too?' she giggled, before they found themselves running back to the car to dodge a shower.

'Probably.' He grinned. 'Although I think he might well have brought the Mercedes on that trip.' And he laughed with her as they scrambled, already soaked, into his car, his conversation as crazy as her own.

He helped her gain confidence in the saddle too, schooling her into being a proficient horsewoman, fortunately without the help of Kay, although Alex knew he still saw the other woman occasionally.

Still, why should she care? she thought, dying inside, nevertheless, when she came back one day from a local charity concert organised by Debbie, Ron's homely, well-rounded, socially-caring wife, only to realise that York had spent the evening with Kay.

Yet in spite of that he took care to ensure that she, Alex, didn't make any real male friends, swiftly dealing with any possible suitors when they went out socially with a possessive arm around her shoulder and a formidable look that had them scurrying away.

'What right do you have to be so possessive?' she challenged one day, after they had been lunching with several of his friends and that usual demonstrative action of his had had one fair-haired young man with whom she had been sharing a joke making a hasty exit she'd felt sure hadn't been planned.

'Exactly that—possession,' he said succinctly, handing her back into the car. 'I believe it's nine tenths of the law.'

'Your law, maybe,' she complained, taking exception to his proprietorial attitude, especially as he seemed to have no real interest in her beyond her being a temporary source of amusement. And as he slid into the driver's seat beside her she reminded him, 'Unfortunately, York, you don't possess me.'

'Unfortunately?' The mocking burn of his glance made her instantly regret her careless choice of words.

'I meant unfortunately for you!'

He laughed at the spots of bright colour tingeing her cheeks before he indicated and pulled away, although his voice was suddenly serious a moment later when he asked, 'What happened to your friend Burrowes?'

If he saw her stiffen, the way her jaw seemed to clench above the smooth ivory of her throat, he didn't say anything. The truth was, though, that she hadn't seen Lonnie since that day he had given her a lift back from town. Perhaps she wouldn't see him again, she prayed silently, feeling the shadows of a tormenting anxiety forming a small, bleak cloud across her spirits, because Lonnie was the one person who could still shatter the fragile bubble of contentment that seemed to surround her these days.

Any response she might have made was too long in coming, and she heard the short, sharp breath York inhaled before he said with sudden, hard impatience, 'Let's take a walk.' Already he had turned the car off the main road, along the narrow street, towards the stretch of moorland high above the town.

'Do I get any choice?' she attempted to say lightly; what she really wanted was to be screaming up the motorway, her destination Heathrow Airport, flying off to the other side of the world, away from him, so that she could begin to deal with the agony of probably never seeing him again. After all, what possible reason could he have for wanting to see her after she had gone?

'No,' was all he said, and then he gave all his concentration to the sharp bend around a war memorial on
the left-hand side of the road, where several young people
were sitting chatting in the late afternoon sun.

The drive to the top was incredible. Typically English
thatched cottages stood sleepily above gardens bright
with alyssum, pansies and forget-me-nots, and, glancing
back across the thatch of one of the houses they had
passed on the hill just below them, Alex could see the
whole resort with the green and gold fields beyond, and,
crowning it all, the breathtaking panorama of the bay.

'It's spectacular,' she whispered, almost to herself, and
knew that she was going to miss this too, this incredible
part of the West Country that she had come to think of
as her own little piece of England.

There was a deep sadness in her eyes as her gaze swept
longingly across the red-roofed houses of the little town,
met the glint of silver water and the sweeping curve of
yellow sand that reached around the coast to the
headland in the distance that was Blue Anchor Bay.

'You haven't ever brought me up here before,' she
commented softly when the road finally levelled off and
York brought the car onto a rough patch of ground that
served as a lay-by. 'It's like being on top of the world.'

'It is—or very close to it,' he said, getting out, his
earlier impatience gone.

Surprisingly, although it was early June and the
holiday season had already started, there was no one
else up here. The moorland hillside was deserted, save
for the two of them.

Alex stood drinking in the view as York locked the
car.

'Come on.'

Casually, as if it was the most natural thing in the
world, he took her hand, looking more relaxed as he
guided her along a stony track, while Alex's every nerve
seemed stretched with anticipation.

'Look.' Oblivious to her tension, it seemed, he pointed out a pyramid of trees to their left with the turrets of a lookout tower on top. 'That's Dunster,' he said. 'If you've been into the old Yarn Market there you might have noticed the hole in one of the rafters where a cannonball was purportedly fired from the castle during the Civil War.'

Alex grimaced, remembering seeing the damage during a visit to the village. 'People don't change, do they?' she remarked wryly, glad to be talking about more mundane things—anything that would take her mind off her totally unwise feelings for York.

'No,' he said in agreement. 'We just use more sophisticated methods these days for blowing each other up.'

But up here it was easy to pretend that there wasn't any turmoil in the world, even if it wasn't so easy to ignore the upheaval going on inside herself; here, where the only sound was of the crickets and the occasional bleat of a sheep. A small yellow butterfly flitted over the short-cropped grass interspersing the track. Gorse, not yet in flower, grew thickly on either side, dark green clumps waving beneath the deep crimson of foxglove and thorny white heads of flowering blackberry.

'Naughty girl,' York admonished softly as she stopped to pluck a buttercup shining glossy yellow in the sun.

'No, I'm not. It's the way to tell if someone's a glutton for butter. Look!' She giggled as she held it under her chin, lifting her head for him to see. 'Am *I*?' Then she wished she hadn't when he pulled her close enough to kiss her throat swiftly, just below where the little flower had cast its bright reflection.

'You should know better than to tease me with little ploys like that,' he said, with an odd reproof behind the laughter. 'If you wanted me to kiss you, all you had to do was ask.'

Oh, God! Why do I love being with him so much? she asked herself desperately, her throat aching so acutely from the touch of his lips that she pulled away, pretending not to care, pretending that his scent, his warmth, his nearness hadn't affected her as she ambled blindly down the hillside in front of him.

BEWARE OF FIRE

Coming upon the seemingly portentous metal sign sticking out of the trees just at that moment, involuntarily Alex shuddered.

Isn't that what I'm doing—playing with fire, she thought, in allowing myself to become so emotionally involved with him?

'It's a reminder—and very necessary,' he said, startling her, because she hadn't realised he was standing right behind her. 'People are careless with camping stoves, matches; even a smouldering cigarette can do it. There are the controlled fires, of course, but that's a different thing altogether. You've probably noticed large areas of burnt heath when we've been on other parts of the moor.'

She nodded. 'Yes, I was wondering about that,' she admitted. 'What's behind the purpose of controlled fires?'

York's smile was indulgent. 'You can tell you've only ever lived in big cities,' he drawled, remembering what she had told him and making it sound as though she had been totally deprived. 'Exmoor's only the way it is because it's managed—managed by a combination of grazing and burning. Heather seed is stimulated by fire,' he went on to explain. 'It starts to age and die off when it reaches about eighteen inches deep, and fire clears the old stuff to promote new. Areas with varying stages of growth are selected so that there's a careful balance of heather left for the wildlife that depend upon each particular stage.'

'And it would be devastating for the wildlife if it weren't,' Alex accepted.

He shrugged. 'It's a fact of life,' he said, glancing at the sign again, 'when people don't care enough to think.'

But you would, she thought automatically, looking at the golden buttercup she was still twirling between her fingers. He would respect nature, from its most glorious to its cruellest aspects.

She didn't need anything else to expand her already overwhelming admiration for him, anything else to make her want him more acutely than she did already.

Carelessly, she swept away from him, walking ahead of him, in silence, through the heath.

'Oh, look, what's that?'

She had stopped by a small wooden structure, half-hidden by trees and shrubs on the lonely hillside—what once might have been a store for forestry tools, but which was derelict now, its door and roof open to the moor and the sky.

Laughing, Alex ran over to it, disappearing inside. Its floor was a carpet of pink heather.

'Ooh, I think I'll move in!' she breathed headily, pivoting so that the rich tones of the multi-print skirt she had teamed with a red blouse moved against her legs in a soft swirl of colour.

York watched from the doorway. Dressed all in navy today, he looked tall and excitingly forbidding. He had to bend his head to come in.

'Well, it might not have a roof or a door—' he pulled a face, unaware of how disturbing she found being with him in the shade of its sun-dappled walls 'but it's certainly a room with a view. Do you recognise it?'

Alex followed his pointing finger to a distinctively tall fir tree in the distance. Behind it were the grey gables and chimneys of a sprawling building, between the last toy-like houses of the town and the patchwork fields. Moorlands!

'I didn't realise you could still see it from here.' She felt his eyes on her, not realising how her features softened at the sight of the proud, elegant house standing in almost blissful isolation against its moorland setting. In fact there was only a farm and one other large house on that, the far side of the town where, away to the west, the softly rolling hills met the thickening forest and the wooded valley. 'You're right. It *is* beautiful,' she whispered.

'Yes,' he agreed sombrely, but he was looking at her, the dark absorption of his gaze making her insides quiver.

She ignored him, fixing her eyes on what was, after all, her family home, though she wasn't really seeing it now, the contours of her face suddenly tense behind the loose waves that shone like polished silver in the sun.

'Up here you must feel like master of all you survey.'

'Mmm,' he agreed, the sound a deep rumble in his throat.

But he was still looking at her, and she uttered shakily, 'I meant the house!'

'Ah.' Fortunately then his gaze followed hers down across the red-roofed houses and the green fields. 'But I'm not, am I?'

Alex looked at him obliquely. 'Not on paper, no.'

'Well, then . . .' She caught her breath as he reached behind her to grasp the doorjamb at her side, his arm accidentally brushing her hair. 'You know . . . it's going to cost me a fortune to buy you out.'

On the gentle breeze her laughter carried some way down the hillside, high-pitched and tremulous.

'You can afford it,' she reminded him blithely, in a voice that nevertheless shook. 'You know, I don't want anything from you,' she appended more seriously after a moment. 'It's yours. It always was—and always will be.' And he didn't know what it cost her as she went on, 'I came over from New Zealand empty-handed, and with the exception of those letters—and a few shares, perhaps—that's the way I intend going back.'

She thought she heard his breath catch. 'You don't have to.'

'What?' She wasn't quite sure what he was getting at.

'Go back.'

Alex's throat worked nervously. What was he suggesting? 'I have to. It's home,' she uttered rather lamely, wishing he weren't making things any harder for her than they already were.

'This is your home, Alexia.' She felt the breath he exhaled, warm against her neck, and gasped as his other arm came down across her breasts, pulling her back against him. 'It always was and always will be,' he said, echoing her own words. 'Your place is here. With me.'

'Wh-what do you mean?' she breathed, closing her eyes at the unbearable pleasure of being held against his hard warmth, her heart thudding so violently that her voice sounded like a croak in her ears.

'What I said.' Roughly he pulled her round to face him, forcing her to meet the inscrutable grey-green of his eyes. 'I mean I want you to stay. Here. In *our* house. With me.'

'You mean ... as we have been?'

She knew he couldn't mean that. Not now. Not when this elemental and overpowering attraction between them was proving too much for either of them to ignore, because something had happened at lunch today to make him finally cross the boundaries of that rigid and daunting self-discipline, and he knew she knew it too, judging by the sound of that almost impatient sigh as he answered, 'No, dearest, not as we have been.'

A wry smile tugged at his mouth. 'I want you in every sense of the word—and I think you know it. I want you to play a far greater role in my life than you've been doing. In my life. In my home. In my bed.'

Until when? The thought screamed through her brain even as she struggled not to accept his unexpected proposition immediately. Loving him as she did, she would be just waiting for the day when he tired of her and found someone else and paid her, his redundant cousin, what he thought was an appropriate price to move out.

'So what have you got to say, darling? Do you think we could make it work permanently?'

'Permanently? You mean...?' Her eyes, desperately searching his, were shining like rain-kissed cornflowers. Outside, somewhere, she was conscious of the faint, tuneful trilling of a skylark. He couldn't be serious. Could he?

'Marry me.' The words issued deeply from his chest. Why, then, did he manage to make it sound more like an order than a request?

She uttered a little laugh, breathless, stunned. 'Marry you?' She couldn't believe that he was actually asking her. 'I can't. I—'

York's other hand clasped her head, his strong fingers tangling in the silver silk. 'Why can't you?' Lines deepened around his eyes and mouth as his gaze raked over the tense contours of her face. 'Is there someone else? This Lonnie chap, perhaps?'

Alex hesitated. Oh, to tell him that there was! To escape from this reckless, impetuous desire to do the one thing she wanted most in the world to do! Because marrying York couldn't be right—for either of them— surely? Too much had gone before. Too much hatred and animosity. And sometimes he still scared her half to death! After a moment, however, she shook her head.

'Well, then,' he said crisply, 'that's settled, then.'

'Is it?' Her palms against the dark cotton of his shirt, she looked up at him doubtfully. He sounded so certain. As certain as she was unsure.

'Yes, my love. You belong to me. You're mine, Alexia.' The possessiveness in his voice sent a tremor along her veins before he crushed her to him, proving it with his kiss.

He hadn't kissed her—not like this—since that day she had visited her grandfather's grave, and desperately she returned his kiss, feeling as though she was burning up in a conflagration of desire. Beneath the urgency of his lips and hands, her doubts took flight. She loved him! Wanted this—more than anything! Wanted nothing better than to be able to call herself York Masterton's wife. Maybe, she admitted silently to herself now, she had wanted it even as a naïve, infatuated adolescent . . .

'Why do you want to marry me, York?' she murmured against the warm flesh of his throat. She still couldn't believe he had asked her, and that it had all been decided without even a word of acceptance from her. 'Is it for my share of the house?' She was anything but serious. 'To save buying me out?'

He chuckled, pressing a tender kiss on the bridge of her nose. 'Why else? It's cheaper this way.' His smile was seductive, the dark fringes of his lashes casting shadows on his cheeks as his gaze lingered on her swollen lips. 'And I get the bonus of having you all to myself— night after night after night.'

The imagery to which his words gave rise sent arrows of need darting down through her lower body, that need escalating as he pulled her hard to him again, his mouth more seeking this time, his fingers twisting roughly in the silver cascade of her hair.

'God, you turn me on!' His breath trembled through him as he groaned against her throat. She could feel the evidence in his hardening body, her own responding as her hips moved provocatively against his in a wanton need to incite him to even further intimacy, and she paid the penalty of her wantonness when he moved to tug open her blouse and expose the warm roundness of her breast.

Her flesh was a pale contrast against the vivid scarlet.

'Like snow against fire . . .'

The sensuality in his voice excited her, the rousing caress of those rough palms against the sensitive peaks of her breasts driving her mindless, so that she wasn't even aware of sliding down with him onto the carpet of heather, their mouths welded, their bodies aching to be one.

She uttered a sharp gasp as his lips found one pale, swollen aureole that was begging for his mouth, and she gritted her teeth in torturous ecstasy as its suckling warmth satisfied one craving and then produced another, hotter and more intense, in the very heart of her femininity.

'Don't stop. Oh, please...' Her fingers tangled in the strength of his hair, holding him down to her when he would have moved away.

'What is it? What do you want?' His voice was a whisper against the pale alabaster of her breast, and even that was exciting her.

She moaned softly, closing her eyes against the depth of her need for him, her hair lying like gossamer silk across the heather, her cheeks touched with the flush of her desire.

'Love me,' she murmured, lost. That was all that would satisfy this eternal hunger for him, she acknowledged wildly, jerking against him as his lips burned feverishly over her ribcage.

The warm hands spanning her tiny waist were unfastening her skirt, easing the colourful fabric down over the gentle curve of her hips, over the smoothness of her thighs, his lovemaking threatening to drive her crazy as he discovered her, bringing into play all his skilled knowledge of a woman's body.

Without even being aware of it she had unfastened his shirt, and now, as he moved above her, her aching fingers caressed the crisp dark hair across his chest, exploring, moving upwards to stroke the warm, smooth velvet of his shoulders.

'Please,' she uttered, wondering when he was going to end this delirium of need in her.

His lips curved in soft satisfaction to hear her begging beneath him. Satisfaction and deep, vulnerable desire, she thought, lifting trembling fingers to his face, caressing the hard curve of his cheek, the slightly rougher texture of his jaw.

'I didn't intend to make love to you here...' She felt his breath shudder through him as her hands slid involuntarily down his body. 'I didn't realise I was quite so capable of losing control so easily.' For a moment a frown knitted those dark brows. 'Do you really want to risk getting pregnant straight away?'

More than anything. I want part of you, she cried silently to him, although she didn't say it. She could only give a soft moan, her face an agony of desire, her body rising with a convulsive movement that said it all.

She didn't remember him undressing, but somehow they were lying on a bed of tangled clothes and heather, their lovemaking as free and natural as the sun that streamed down out of the blue above them, the sounds of their passion mingling with the skylark's song.

And when he took her at last, though she hadn't found a way to tell him that he was her first and only lover, or the reason why she was still a virgin at twenty-seven, her body accepted him as readily and painlessly as if life had schooled her for this one moment—to be part of York—so that she was crying from sheer joy and love and relief as the intensity of their mutual climax ebbed away.

A long time afterwards, with laughter in his voice, he said, 'We'd better get married quickly. Just in case. Is there anyone you particularly want to invite?'

'No.' She had a few friends, but no one close enough to warrant dragging them twelve thousand miles across the world. 'Just as long as you're there.' She smiled up into the strong perfection of his face, her eyes moist and sparkling, wondering how it all could possibly have happened.

'Try stopping me,' he breathed, his hands unintentionally arousing again as they gently fondled her naked body, that forceful determination, which was an integral part of his character, penetrating his shuddering words.

That he was wildly, wholly besotted, Alex was in no doubt. She could see it in his eyes, in the tremor with which emotion filled his voice. And in the days that followed he proved it to her—in his constant demands to have her near him, in tender looks, and with lovemaking that neither of them could get enough of.

He's mine. To have and to hold, she thought, the night before the wedding, hugging her pleasure to herself as, from Edmundo's beautifully tended garden, she gazed up at the moor above the resort, packed with tourists now for the summer. The spot on that hillside where they had pledged their lives to each other would always be special to her, she thought with a soft, secretive smile, and could see nothing to mar her happiness in the age-old phrase that rang automatically through her brain. 'For better for worse...'

CHAPTER EIGHT

JOYCE STERN was waiting by the front door to greet them as they pulled up on the cobbled forecourt.

Tanned and glowing and happy, holding hands as they came into the hall, they had to look a picture of contentment, Alex thought blissfully, smiling across at York in the secret exchange of glances that was reserved for lovers and which encapsulated all the joy and love and ecstasy they had enjoyed during their month-long honeymoon, island-hopping in the South Pacific.

They had spent some time in New Zealand too, so that she could terminate the lease on her flat, arrange for shipment of her belongings, visit one or two of her friends. They had been green with envy, she remembered, when she had introduced York as her husband.

'I've put your post and your papers in the study, sir, and the water's hot if Alex...I mean Mrs Masterton...would like a bath.'

'Thank you, Joyce.' York put an arm around Alex, his smouldering eyes turning her legs to jelly as he smiled down at her and without so much as a glance back at the housekeeper uttered, 'But I think we'll both take that bath.'

'Very good, sir.'

It was such a stiff, emotionless response to what her employer clearly had in mind that Alex couldn't contain a giggle.

'You're wicked!' she whispered at him as they started up the stairs.

'Yes.' His grin was a flash of white in his darkly tanned face. 'And don't you just love it?' he reminded her.

Yes, I do, her heart sang. He had made their past four weeks together wildly exciting and rapturous, had

promised her that things would never change. And he
meant to see to it that they didn't, she recognised with
a little thrill as she was undressing a few minutes later
in the luxurious bedroom that they would be sharing.

It was a large room with an *en suite* bathroom, and
running the depth of the house, it offered views over
both the front drive and the rear gardens. They had
planned its decor together, in creams and apricots and
rich mahogany, and Joyce had made sure that all the
decorations and furnishings had been completed before
their return, Alex realised gratefully, her fingers un-
steady as they slipped the buttons on her simple, floral
tea-dress.

When the phone shrilled beside the huge four-poster
bed, she went automatically across to answer it. York
was in the bathroom and the taps were running, so he
probably wouldn't hear it in there.

'So how's the blushing bride? Or should I say, how
are the kissing cousins?' Alex's spirits plummeted as she
heard Lonnie's mocking drawl coming down the line.

'You choose the most inopportune moments, Lonnie,'
she breathed, low enough so that York wouldn't be likely
to hear. 'We've only just got back.' And, angry that he
was continuing to contact her in spite of knowing how
she felt about him, she added, 'I don't suppose you've
considered that your call might not be particularly
welcome?'

Soft laughter followed the briefest silence. 'Never. You
know you don't mean that, sweetheart. I'll catch you
some other time.'

Don't bother! she was about to snap back, hating him
for the uneasy feeling his call had resurrected in her, but
he had already rung off.

She was dropping the phone onto its cradle as York
came back into the bedroom. He was wearing only a
towel around his loins, and just the sight of his superbly
tanned body caused a familiar ache in the pit of
Alex's stomach.

'Someone ringing us already?'

'It was no one,' she murmured, feeling somehow guilty, not wanting to taint their first day home by dragging up Lonnie's name. She remembered how furious York had been when he'd seen the other man driving away from the house that day. 'No one for us,' she added, which was the truth.

That high forehead creased as though he'd detected her slight hesitancy in answering him. He said nothing, however, as he came across and took her in his arms, and a moment later she was giving herself up to him in desperate abandon as his kiss drove Lonnie Burrowes and everything else from her mind.

Life had never been sweeter, Alex thought as she finished that morning's task of starting to decorate one of the smaller bedrooms, admiring the new landing curtains as she passed them, and the deeper shades on the wall-lamps—small changes she had been making generally around the home.

Home. She lingered over the word as delightfully as she reflected on the six blissful weeks of her marriage. It had taken everyone by surprise—friends, neighbours, Celia—when York had announced news of the quiet, register-office wedding that was to take place, only three weeks after he had proposed.

Now, this morning, a Welsh dresser had arrived from a famous London store—a late wedding present from Celia—and afterwards Alex had had a long chat over the phone with her mother-in-law in Ireland, before that other exciting call had come through. And, to add to all that, York—who had been away for a few days—was coming home tonight. Consequently, she was whistling a little tune under her breath as she went into the bedroom and stripped off the T-shirt and jeans she had been wearing to work in.

She was just crossing to the wardrobe to find something fresh to put on when a knock on the open door made her turn, surprised.

Joyce was in town, shopping, so who...?

'Well, well. When old Pedro told me you were inside I didn't realise I'd find you so delightfully attired.'

Lonnie was leaning against the doorjamb, leering with unashamed insolence at the pink satin camisole and French knickers which were all Alex was standing in.

'How did you get in?' she demanded inhospitably, shocked, as well as taking exception to his disrespectful reference to their gardener.

'The door was open,' he said, with a casual gesture. 'When I couldn't find you downstairs I came to the natural conclusion that you had to be upstairs.' His tone was more than mildly sarcastic. 'I must say, marriage seems to be agreeing with you.' His appreciation of her full, high breasts beneath the scalloped pink satin was more than uncomfortably blatant. 'Your master keeping you well and truly satisfied?'

'What do you want?' she challenged, ignoring his overtly suggestive remark.

'What I've always wanted.' His shoulder moved under the loose, fashionable suit as he came away from the door. 'A night in bed with you. Oh, don't worry...' he put up a hand as though in defence against the sudden fearful challenge glittering in her eyes '...I know when to concede defeat. I'm not a poor loser. I'll just have to be content with a mere story.'

Alex looked at him obliquely. 'A story?' Wariness clouded her eyes simply at the knowledge of how unscrupulous Lonnie could be. 'What about?'

He smiled, his lips moist—too full, she had always thought. 'Oh, nothing sordid. Just a line or two as to what it felt like to come home. Your version of why you stayed away so long. Whether it was love at first sight with that immensely rich cousin of yours. The whirlwind romance thing. You know. You've worked on a paper. Readers like things like that.'

'Get lost.'

He laughed. 'Oh, come on, Alex! I could, but then I'd have to rely on memory to provide me with some story about you, and while the facts as I know them might do wonders for the rag I don't think that husband of yours would be too pleased reading about them. Having a slur like that hanging over the family name's one thing—marrying it quite another. Or haven't you told him?'

A thud in the next room made her dart a glance sideways as she remembered Denise. Denise came in during the week to clean and, sweet though she was, loved to talk.

Oh, dear God... 'You'd better come in,' she whispered, feeling defeated.

He sauntered into the room, smug as a jockey who'd just cleared the first hurdle, she thought, her skin crawling.

'Very nice.' He turned from admiring the magnificent room, those too-blue eyes appraising her as she stood there looking unwittingly seductive with her hair tousled, in nothing but her satin underwear, against the closed door. 'Holy...!' His eyes were undressing her, feasting, hungry. 'You must drive him mad!'

Quickly, Alex made a grab for the black negligée that was lying on the bed, recoiling from the brush of Lonnie's arm against hers as he snatched it out of her grasp, holding it behind his back.

'No, I think I'd prefer to interview you like this.' His mouth had turned ugly. 'At least that way you won't be so bloody arrogant,' he breathed, then let out a coarse laugh. She thought she smelt alcohol on his breath.

Heaven! How she wished she had never laid eyes on him! Never confided in him as a lonely, tortured adolescent ...

The interview was brief. Sitting on the bed, hating every aspect of it from that repulsive masculine presence to the cheap, cloying aftershave, she answered most of his questions without revealing anything too personal, keeping her replies as economical as she could.

'There,' he said, pocketing his pencil and his notebook after what seemed to Alex like fifteen minutes of solid purgatory. 'That didn't hurt in any way, did it? And, for your co-operation, sweetheart, put this around your shoulders. I wouldn't want you to get cold.'

So when the door opened she was clutching the black silk she had snatched from him against her revealing camisole, looking towards the door in horrified dismay.

'York!'

'What the hell's going on?'

His face was an agony of bewildered disbelief as he looked first at Alex, then Lonnie, and back to Alex again. Vaguely she was aware that Lonnie had managed to put a degree of distance between himself and York, and for once in his life he looked scared.

'Ask your wife. She invited me in here.' Unbelievably he was incriminating her with his usual audacity, despite the violence of York's pulsing anger. 'Go on—ask her.'

He didn't. The glowering mask of his face said only too clearly what he believed.

'Get out of here, Burrowes, before I throw you down the stairs head first!' His fists clenched, it was clear he had every intention of doing just that, but as he made a move towards the other man Lonnie bolted like a petrified fox going to ground.

'York...it isn't what you think.' Desperate to convince him, Alex made a move to get up. 'I—'

'Stay where you are!' She shrank away from his savage command as he took a few threatening steps towards her. 'I want to see what a cheating wife looks like while she's still fresh from her lover's arms!'

Oh, God! He couldn't really believe... 'It isn't like that!' It was almost a sob.

'No?' His laugh was cold and harsh. 'Tell me what it's like, Alexia. Does he have you begging like I do?'

'Stop it!' Her hands clamped over her ears but roughly he dragged them down.

'Exactly how long has this been going on? Since before we were married?' His fingers bit into her wrist, hurting her with their trembling strength. 'Or is it just something that's happened since?'

'No! I'm not having an affair with him!' She had to make him believe her—make him understand.

'No? Then just what would you call it?'

Of course. What else could he imagine? Her face was lined with tortured appeal against the hard, raw anger of his. 'York, please . . .'

'Yes, we've been there often enough, haven't we?' His mockery of the sobbing creature to which he could reduce her within the privacy of their lovemaking cut into her, deep and wounding. 'It's just as well I caught an early train so that I could see just what my pretty little wife gets up to while I'm away. Wasn't what we had enough for you, Alexia?'

Behind the darkness of his anger she could almost feel his clawing, ravaging pain.

'What about all we've shared? All those times we . . . God!' Roughly he pushed her back onto the bed and stood there staring down at her, his features contorted with rage and hurt and sickening disenchantment. 'Just how much more exactly does a man have to give?'

The words seemed wrenched from him, stabbing Alex to the heart.

'I told you. It's not like that.' It was a small, desperate endeavour to break through his torturing anger, but his suspicion was too deep, his pain too intense to be reasoned with as he cut across her hopeless attempts to explain.

'What did you think I was—some sort of bloody fool! What have I been—just a source of amusement to you, Alexia? A diversion from your sleazy friend Burrowes?

Or just a meal-ticket while you carried on your squalid little affair behind my back?'

'Surely you don't need to ask?' she uttered, aching for him even in her abject misery. 'You know what you mean to me—'

'Do I?' His anger was unremitting. 'And just how many times have you told Burrowes the same thing?'

'I haven't! I mean...'

What could she tell him, other than the truth? But it lay locked, like a slumbering tormentor, in the recesses of her mind, so that words wouldn't come and she flinched as she heard him say resignedly, 'Don't try to deny it, dearest. You'll just be making fools of both of us.' Hard lines etched his face, making him look drawn, suddenly older. 'And I thought you were something special...' Bitterness vied with the pain in his eyes, twisting his mouth into an ugly line as he swung disgustedly away.

'York, don't. Please! Don't do this to us. York...' It was a small, sobbing plea for his understanding, and, knowing now that only one thing would restore him to reason, bring him back to her, she uttered on a note of desperation, 'I'm pregnant.'

She hadn't intended to tell him like this. She'd planned a romantic dinner with music and candles, and when he stopped dead, turned round and stared at her as though somehow he hadn't comprehended, she murmured desolately, 'I'm pregnant. I'm going to have a baby.'

Shock manifested itself on his face, an emotion so profound that for several seconds he seemed unable to move; shock and something else momentarily softened his features, causing him to take a step towards her, put a deep, questioning line between his eyes. Then it was gone, replaced by something she saw only as lacerating anguish before a cold mask came down over his features and unbelievably he breathed, 'So whose is it? Mine or his?'

She couldn't even credit that he was saying this! 'How dare you?' Her breasts rose on a convulsive sob torn from her by his accusation when she had thought it would make him happy. But, of course, she should have realised...

'Was that why you didn't hesitate when I asked you to marry me—because you were already pregnant? Was it?' His body was rigid with censure and suspicion as he moved back to her. 'Was that why you were so quick to assure me that you wanted a family right away?'

Was that what he thought? Sitting up, she could only gaze up at his dark-suited figure, her eyes wide and tormented, while he went on, his tongue inexorably flaying her, destroying them, torturing them both.

'What was wrong? Wouldn't he marry you? Is that why you were so keen to accept *my* offer? What were you hoping—that you could pass off any child as mine and I'd never know the truth?'

'If you think like that,' she sobbed, pulling up the strap of her camisole which had slipped alluringly off her shoulder, 'then I'll go. I'm not staying here to be treated like...like...'

'Like what?' Anger drew his lips back into a snarl. 'Like a first-rate little harlot?'

She dragged in a breath, reeling from his unbearable remarks, and inside her something seemed to uncoil and snap, those last cruel words, although spoken in the heat of the moment, hurting her more than he could ever know.

'I can't prove it isn't mine, can I?' he went on, lancing into her pride and her dignity and her selfless, excruciating love for him. 'In which case, for the time being, you're going to do exactly as I say.

'There's no way you're going to stir up any sort of scandal in this family the way your mother tried to do. You're going to stay here and play the dutiful, loving wife until I decide otherwise and until such time as I think it's a respectable enough period for you to do anything else. In the meantime you can enjoy the luxury of my money, my company, and my share of this house, but don't expect anything else from me, Alexia, because you've taken the last of everything I'll ever have to give!'

And with that he strode out, banging the door hard behind him.

Flinging herself back onto the bed, Alex buried her face in the pale satin, too hurt even to cry.

How could this have happened, just when she had thought that after all the earlier doubt and suspicion she had won his love, had created the perfect marriage, when she had planned the perfect evening for them both, had been so excited about the baby? She had nearly phoned him as soon as the surgery had rung her to confirm that the result of her test was positive, but she had forced herself to wait, wanting to make it special. And now...

The irony of the situation didn't strike her then. Only later did it dawn upon her that, just as he had doubted her own identity in the beginning, he was now questioning the very identity of their child.

Over the next few weeks, as a hot, dry August turned into an even hotter September, they lived like comparative strangers. York spent a lot of time away, sometimes only returning to Moorlands at weekends.

On several occasions during those desperately awaited visits from her husband, Alex attempted to convince him that there had been nothing in that scene he had witnessed between her and Lonnie Burrowes, but he refused to listen and, as she couldn't bear to tell him the real reason why she had thought fit, in her semi-naked state, to admit the reporter into her bedroom, eventually she gave up even bothering to try. Sometimes she endeavoured to convince herself that if York had really cared anything for her he would have trusted her enough to believe her, and yet at other times she wondered if, had it been the other way around and she had found him in the same compromising position, she would have found it any easier to believe him.

Those deliriously happy days of their early marriage had gone. He no longer shared her bed, had moved out of their room the night of that dreadful afternoon when he had found her with Lonnie, since when he had left her entirely alone. He did, nevertheless, demand that she accompany him to any social and professional functions he was obliged to attend—the company's summer ball in London, a conference in Paris, a local garden party where he was guest of honour—but she knew it was out of nothing more than his desire to protect the family name.

Beside him, though she didn't know it, she appeared wan but surprisingly serene, and if anyone noticed the tension in either of them—in Alex's fragile beauty or in the taut hardness of York's face—then no one said a word.

Sometimes she wondered why she didn't just leave. He couldn't have done anything, she assured herself, if she had. It might have raised a few eyebrows, given rise to speculation, but it would have blown over eventually. The only plausible reason she could offer herself for staying was that she loved him.

And that is your own stupid misfortune, she thought miserably, because in spite of everything he still made her pulses leap, his hard masculinity calling to that quintessential part of her womanhood that made her want to feast her eyes on him, unable to absorb enough of him. And that was how she felt one morning, as he strode into the dining room with his usual air of forceful vitality and tossed a tabloid he'd usually never have considered worth reading down on to the table.

'Congratulations. You've managed to make second-page news! I'm not particularly interested in what you're getting up to with that no-good boyfriend of yours, but I do draw the line at seeing my name dragged into a gutter-raking rag like this! What the hell did you think you were playing at?'

Sitting there in her negligée, Alex stared down at the newspaper, folded roughly at the relevant page. The article was headed KISSIN' KOUSINS. There was nothing too destructive about it. It was merely a dressed-up story of her return from New Zealand and their recent wedding, doctored—Lonnie Burrowes style—to make it as cheap and gossipy as possible. There was a photograph of them too, taken at some recent charity function.

'I told you he wanted a story.' She looked up at him, her face pale, her eyelids heavy. 'You weren't here—and there was no other way I could get him to go.'

'What was wrong with simply ordering him out? Or was that impossible since he was already in your bed?'

Alex dropped her gaze to the table, with its fine silverware laid for the breakfast that her morning sickness had made it impossible to stomach. She wasn't feeling up to another slanging match with him today.

'Did you tell him to slant it well enough to look like your marriage was a suitable atonement for what your childhood and illegitimacy deprived you of? Is that why you married me, *dearest*?'

She groaned as she finished reading that final paragraph, another wave of sickness threatening to wash over her as she thought about what Lonnie *could* have written, but all she said was, 'Think what you like, York.'

Wretchedly she pushed her plate aside, struggling to her feet.

'Yes, it does rather leave a nasty taste in one's mouth, doesn't it?' he breathed with unrelenting censure as his gaze fell on her untouched breakfast. 'What is it—lovesickness? Or aren't you—?'

She caught his sudden expletive as she clutched the edge of the table, breathing deeply to try and alleviate the dizzying sickness, heard his subsequent whispered, 'My God! You look awful!'

Compared with you, she thought, I probably do. He looked fit and hard and dynamic.

'Perhaps it's because we've created a baby! Ever thought about that?' she uttered, feeling faint, wondering, as she made to pass him, if she was ever going to make it to the door. 'We're having a baby, and only one of us is having to face responsibility for it...'

She would have stumbled then if he hadn't caught her. Through an orange haze she heard the soft oath he uttered, felt his arm go around her, his hand splayed across her midriff, so that she leaned back against him for a second, needing him, needing his tenderness, his hard, supportive strength.

'Don't worry—I shan't let you down this afternoon,' she got out, her breathing coming rather laboriously. They had been invited to a local fund-raising affair in aid of mentally handicapped children, to which, she had been surprised to discover, York had magnanimously donated an extremely generous cheque. 'I wouldn't dream of allowing your child ever to stop me from being the perfect wife,' she uttered with all the bitter sarcasm she could manage.

But he had swept her up in his arms, his voice firm yet strangely hoarse as he rasped, 'You aren't going anywhere.'

A small, muffled protest rose from her lips. As he carried her upstairs she wanted to free herself from the devastating effects his warmth, strength and those sure, steady arms were having upon her, but she couldn't. She could only lie there with her head against his shoulder, feeling the soft fabric of his jacket against her cheek.

I love you! her heart cried as her aching senses absorbed the hard warmth of him that seemed to be engulfing her, the dark shading of his jaw so close to her lips, the sweet familiarity of his aftershave.

'York...'

'Get some rest,' he said, still with that strangely husky voice, ignoring her poignant whisper as he straightened

from placing her on the bed, covering her with the duvet.
'I'll look in on you later.'

But he didn't. Or, at least, not while she was awake,
because when she opened her eyes again the sun
streaming into the room told her that it was already well
into the afternoon and that York would have left for the
fête.

As if in confirmation, she heard his car purr to life
beneath her window, then those powerful tyres whis-
pering over the drive.

Quickly she got out of bed, hungering for the smallest
glimpse of him, and saw only Kay's dark Range Rover
parked there on the forecourt. So he must have telephoned Kay to tell her that she, Alex, wasn't well, and
had taken the other woman instead!

Pain, resentment and anger burned inside her. How
could he? she wondered desolately.

Very easily, a little voice inside her responded, if he
thinks you're having an affair with Lonnie Burrowes.

Which he does, she accepted hopelessly, and then, on
a surge of angry adrenalin, decided that she would take
steps to change it. And right now, she resolved, picking
up the phone—and a moment later she was being put
through to Lonnie's office.

'So what did you want me to do? Convince York
Masterton we're not seeing each other?' Giving his request for a *crème brûlée* to the waiter, who disappeared
after Alex shook her head to indicate that she didn't
want dessert, Lonnie laughed. 'He wouldn't altogether
believe that if he walked in here now.'

Alex shuddered. She didn't want to be here, having
lunch in this prestigious London hotel with Lonnie. She
had wanted to get their talk over with in his office; that
was what she had been hoping when she had telephoned
him the previous day, but today he had insisted on
bringing her here before he would discuss a thing.

'For heaven's sake, Lonnie, this isn't a joking matter!'
From her tone, the sparks dancing in her eyes, he had
to realise she was desperate.

'No, it isn't,' he agreed, glancing over his shoulder to
where the waiter was already striding back with his
dessert. 'Although it certainly doesn't say much for the
blushing bride if she can't convince her husband herself.
I must say, he looks the possessive type—and inordi-
nately jealous!' He surveyed her, head at an angle. 'Does
he beat you as well?' he enquired smoothly, ignoring the
man who was placing his *crème brûlée* in front of him.

Alex gave him a withering look, uncomfortably aware
of the waiter, who was much too well-trained in his profession to display any sign of having overheard.

'I must confess I rather like the idea of Masterton
thinking I'm carrying on with his wife,' Lonnie remarked smugly after the waiter had left them again. 'I'm
sure it must be a new experience for him, with all that
sophistication and money, thinking that there's one
woman—and not just any woman but the one he
married—looking for her excitement with someone else!
Most of the women he's been involved with that I've
read about seemed ready to sell their souls to stay in his
bed!'

'Lonnie!' She didn't want to know about this. That
he was jealous of York was obvious.

'I'm sorry, sweetheart,' he said, popping a spoonful
of the dark, caramelised custard into his mouth, 'but
with this one I'm afraid you're on your own. If you
can't convince him of your own fidelity, then, I'm sorry,
but that's something you're gonna have to work out by
yourself. I'm not risking being flattened by a jealous
husband—he's got twice the muscle I've got and a lethal
temper to match, as we both know.

'It was unfortunate he came in and caught me in your
room that day, but, as I said, it's your marriage, you've
got to sort it out. Unless, of course, you've given him

other reasons to doubt your undying devotion to him, like not keeping his bed warm for him when he's away.

'I know I shouldn't drag this up, but sometimes the past can leave deeper marks on us than we realise, especially when we're young and impressionable. Sometimes it isn't always easy not to fall into the same trap...' She watched him spooning up his dessert, her throat clogging, sick to her stomach. 'You know, you really should have had this. It's delicious. Nice and cool for a hot day like today.'

Alex stared at him, speechless, unable to believe what he was saying, wishing she hadn't humbled herself by coming here and asking him to help her. That he wasn't going to was probably par for the course. She might have expected it. But to actually bring up the one terrible scar on her past, the most painful thing in her life, which nine years ago had dragged her down into such a depression that she had been forced to confide in someone... Anyone. She could have chosen anyone. But she'd chosen this conscienceless individual sitting across the table.

'You're despicable!' she breathed, knocking the table as she stumbled to her feet. And this was all because she had bruised that sensitive male ego by refusing to go out with him, condemned his code of ethics as a suddenly enlightened nineteen-year-old—all those years ago!

'No, I'm not. I'm just being practical. Practical and analytical,' he expanded, unperturbed by what she had called him. But she wasn't listening, hardly even heard his sudden curious, 'What's wrong?'

She was standing riveted to the spot by the sight of two women, who had just got up from a table across the room and were weaving their way towards the main exit—one, a tall blonde she had never seen before, the other, small and pretty with short dark hair and dark flashing eyes that suddenly turned in her direction. Kay Weatherby!

'Oh, God,' Alex groaned under her breath.

CHAPTER NINE

'WHAT'S wrong?' Lonnie was asking again, and with that infuriatingly amused tone jeered, 'Someone you know and wish you didn't?'

Her heart plummeting in dismay, Alex couldn't answer. She wasn't sure whether Kay had noticed her or not. The woman had shown no sign of surprise—or recognition—but she couldn't have failed to see her.

As Kay and her companion disappeared through the door under the exit sign, Alex looked accusingly at Lonnie.

'You knew, didn't you?' she breathed, her detestation of him apparent in her anguished blue eyes. 'That's why you brought me here—insisted on this particular restaurant...'

'I swear to God...' He laid a hand on his heart, trying to look innocent; she had to admit he would have worn the same triumphant expression even if he hadn't planned it, just at seeing her so nonplussed.

'Was it someone who's likely to tell *Yorkie* she saw us together?' he sneered, making Alex recoil and realise how much he must despise her. Had he wanted her that much nine years ago?

At the moment, however, that was the least of her worries. She didn't know if he had deliberately engineered this meeting with Kay, or even if he knew the woman. He would probably gloat over anything he thought might put her marriage into further jeopardy.

It might all have been a dreadful coincidence, she realised, but didn't stay to listen to anything else he had to say. She had to get out of there. And now. She would take a cab back to the station and hope that if Kay had, by some miracle, not actually noticed her there with Lonnie in the restaurant she didn't bump into her in the street. If the woman hadn't seen her but then saw her outside, she might still tell York in passing, and, guilty as Alex was feeling at that moment over even being with Lonnie, she knew that York would start to wonder what she was doing in London, might even put two and two together . . .

But if Kay *had* already seen her, and she made it her business to tell York, then Alex knew that whatever hope she had of ever convincing him that there was nothing between her and the journalist would be dashed for good.

The following day at least was busy enough to take her mind off her immediate worries.

York had arranged a barbecue for the benefit of those business colleagues and acquaintances who were insisting on his throwing a party to introduce his new wife, and just the thought of the evening was nerve-racking enough for Alex without her harbouring any anxieties about Kay.

The day turned into another of the hot, sunny days that they had been experiencing for weeks; it was an unexpectedly glorious summer that had brought a drought and turned the familiar green of the surrounding countryside to an uncharacteristic gold, bleaching the fields and hills almost white in parts from the long dry spell.

By seven o'clock the day still hadn't lost any of its stifling heat and, in a strapless red cocktail dress and with her hair swept up, emphasising the ivory of her neck and slender back, Alex wandered out onto the lawn below the terrace, where tables and chairs and trestle-tables laid with salads and bread and jugs of deliciously cool punch had been positioned.

Casting an efficient eye over them, she gave a last order to one of the caterers.

Playing the perfect hostess as York had wanted, she thought achingly, grateful at least that because of the barbecue he was going to be at home tonight—even if she had to share him with everyone else, and even if he *had* only arranged this evening to show his colleagues, friends and neighbours that, ostensibly at least, they were the perfect couple.

Well, she wouldn't disappoint him! she thought in a suddenly rash mood, plastering on a smile; and only she knew the reason for that mysteriously dark emotion in her eyes as she turned her gaze from the tables to the backdrop of prominent moorland that dominated the town.

She frowned, her concentration held by something halfway up the hillside. A thin coil of smoke was rising above a patch of dark green gorseland, curling stealthily upwards into the evening sky.

She knew, of course. She just needed someone else to spell it out for her. But even as the caterer who was stacking plates paused to follow her anxious gaze to where she was pointing a deep, concerned voice at her shoulder suddenly whispered, 'Oh, hell!'

York had come up unexpectedly behind them, his presence seeming to dominate the scene as always, and Alex felt that unwelcome rush of excitement she always experienced whenever she saw him, her gaze tugging with aching awareness over the dark elegance of his suit that was tailormade for his superb body, over the sleekness of his hair and those clean-cut, angular features.

'Will it come to anything?' Striving against her body's traitorous responses to that lethal animal magnetism, she nevertheless looked and sounded as concerned as he had.

'It's a pretty dead cert. We haven't had any rain for weeks. Everything's so dry that the whole hillside will probably go up like tissue-paper. All we can do is hope it's been reported in time for it not to get too far out of hand.' He sent a swift glance to the caterer who was making a last, hasty check of the tables. 'Is everything under control?'

'Yes, Mr Masterton. Thanks to your very capable wife here.' The man was beaming appreciatively at Alex over the rims of his spectacles. A man probably in his fifties, he added with harmless envy to York, 'You're a very lucky man.'

'Aren't I?' Something cold and flaying echoed in the deep tones, but in the hooded eyes resting on Alex there was an unfathomable emotion that brought her chin up in fragile defiance and locked their glances in silent combat for a few moments.

Fortunately, however, the first guests had started to arrive. But Alex's relief was short-lived when she noticed that Kay was among them.

Without an escort, in a short emerald-green dress that flattered her dark hair and revealed just a little too much of her slight, boyish figure, Kay had quite apparently dressed solely with the intention of gaining York's interest tonight. It didn't help to lessen her suspicions either when, with a waft of subtly expensive perfume, she came straight up to kiss him on the cheek, standing on tiptoe to do so, her well-manicured, red-tipped nails resting on his dark sleeve as she murmured, 'What have you been doing lately, York? Working too hard as usual? I rang you yesterday—early—very early—before I went off to London—' she flashed an uncomfortably perceptive smile at Alex '—but you both seemed to be away.'

A knot seemed to tighten in the middle of Alex's chest. Was Kay testing her? Had she actually noticed her in that hotel restaurant with Lonnie?

'Really?' A furrow brought those thick, masculine brows together. 'I'm not always around during the week, Kay—you know that. But Alexia should have been here...' There was a query in the grey-green eyes that tugged with smouldering assessment over Alex. 'You aren't the best of people to get out of bed in the mornings.'

'He speaks from experience,' Kay uttered with a knowing little laugh. 'Anyway, York, who can blame her?'

'Where were you?' he pressed quietly, choosing to ignore the way the other woman's eyes seemed to be undressing him, her innuendo being that if she were married to him *she* wouldn't want to get up either.

'Very probably still in bed if it was that early.' Alex laughed, her tone light, hiding nerves. 'Otherwise I was probably already off somewhere shopping.' And even that was a lie, she thought, hating herself, because she had had nothing on her mind yesterday when she had travelled up to London but confronting Lonnie Burrowes. But how could she say, I went to see Lonnie, to try and make him convince you how much I love you? She couldn't. She shrugged. 'I made a day of it,' she uttered, compounding the lie.

'Lucky girl!' Kay smiled, though there was a line between her dark, intelligent eyes that made Alex's stomach muscles contract with excruciating tension. 'I wish I had a husband who would put up with me spending his money from the crack of dawn till dusk. But then you've got a fathomless supply, haven't you, York?'

His hard mouth quirked in sardonic amusement. 'Not one that could necessarily stand your spending power, Kay. Alexia, I'm happy to say, is rather more prudent.'

He was standing up for her? She felt a trickle of warmth start to permeate her blood and thought, Oh, you hopeless, hopeless fool!

'You mean in her spending?' Was she imagining it, or could she hear, through her idiotic pleasure, the silent accusation Kay was making—an accusation that screamed, She wasn't being particularly prudent or discreet in London yesterday? Her nerves were stretched taut as the woman turned to her with a blazing smile and said, 'York hasn't said as much in so many words, but I believe congratulations are in order.'

'Oh?' Alex looked frowningly towards York, but he had already excused himself and was moving away to welcome several more guests who had just arrived.

'He indicated that you were being sick all over the place and dropping off at all hours of the day,' Kay enlarged, in response to Alex's stunned enquiry. 'That's why you didn't come to the fête the other day, isn't it? You're pregnant, aren't you?'

Beneath the striking scarlet of Alex's dress, it hadn't even begun to show.

'It isn't common knowledge yet, Kay,' she uttered, adding quickly, 'I've never liked the idea of broadcasting these things too soon in case something goes wrong.'

Kay made a cynical sound. 'What could?' He could find out you're seeing another man! those glittering brown eyes seemed to be saying. 'You're both reasonably young and healthy—even if you aren't the ideal age for a first-time mum.' It seemed she just had to slip that in unnecessarily. 'So when is it due? March? April?'

This time Alex wasn't imagining the unspoken question—the jealousy—behind the beautiful oval face. Were you already pregnant when he married you? Is that how you managed to land him? And the irony of it was that York thought so too, she reminded herself painfully before she murmured, 'Something like that.'

Kay suddenly startled her by commenting, 'You want it all, don't you? This lovely house. York. A baby. In which case I'd strongly advise you to hang onto it for all you're worth because, I'm telling you now, one slip of the reins, Alexia Masterton, and I'll be there without any qualms to take him away from you.'

The blatant admission caused Alex's breath to catch. The smell of sizzling steak, wafting towards them on a cloud of blue smoke from the terrace, should have made her mouth water but made her feel decidedly queasy instead.

'Is that why you don't care about flirting with him in public even though he's married?' she challenged pointedly.

Kay shrugged. 'Why not? He was mine before he was ever yours.'

Her bitterness was tangible as, tight-lipped, she glanced over her shoulder, recognised someone she knew and turned away, leaving Alex entirely shaken from the little episode.

Had she seen her with Lonnie yesterday? Was that why she felt confident enough to issue that threat? Or did Kay know that York's marriage was already on the rocks, which was why she seemed bent on using those incalculable charms of hers to seduce him back into her arms? Well, tonight Kay was going to be out of luck, Alex determined, if she thought that she was just going to hand her husband over—like a barbecued spare-rib—on a plate! Wasn't it her right—and her duty, she thought with a resolve that gave an aloof beauty to her features—to fight for the man she loved?

Where the other guests were concerned, however, it must have looked as though fighting for him was the last thing she needed to do. Because tonight, she realised, as the warm day slipped into a sultry, scented evening, York was being outwardly attentive. And even if she knew it was for the exclusive benefit of everyone present she couldn't help trembling as they were talking to Ron and his wife and York's hand strayed with almost abstracted idleness across the smooth ivory of her back.

Nothing he did, though, was ever done idly or without cool, studied purpose, she thought, hardly listening to whatever it was that Debbie was saying. Was he therefore

merely trying to give the right impression to his guests?
Or was he trying to assess how responsive she might still
be to him? she wondered with a traitorous little frisson.
Was he playing with her emotions for his own typically
masculine satisfaction?

'Hey, look at that!'

Nearby, someone shouted above the hubbub of
laughter and conversation rippling across the terrace and
the lawn, and all eyes suddenly seemed riveted on the
range of moorland above the town, the comments
coming thick and fast.

'Crikey!'

'What do they usually do in these circumstances?'

'It was just a spiral of smoke when we left home!'

How long ago that had been, Alex wasn't sure, but
since she'd spotted the ominous smoke when she'd been
talking to the caterer earlier the wind had fanned the
smouldering bracken to life and small flames were
creeping along the hillside, like a river of glowing crimson
in the dusk.

'It's really starting to spread now!'

Alex turned away as someone spoke at her shoulder,
a plumpish, middle-aged woman whose name she had
forgotten since York had introduced her earlier.

'I think you've done wonders with the house, dear.
Page was a poppet but he didn't have a clue about
making a place welcoming. But you and York—you've
really made it a home!'

Painfully, Alex forced her lips into an appreciative
smile. If only you knew! she thought.

'I was just talking to Kay Weatherby...' The woman
leaned a little closer, her voice growing more intimate—
confidential. 'She's such a sweet gel—and rather fond
of York, I think, at one time...' Rather tactlessly she
went on, 'And she just happened to hint that we might
be hearing the patter of tiny feet around here in
the spring.'

How gossip travels! Like wildfire! Alex thought with an ironical little grimace, a small, forced laugh detracting from the sadness in her eyes.

'Possibly, but I'd hoped we'd cured the mouse problem,' she couldn't help responding flippantly, because she guessed that the woman was pretty thick with Kay and, just like her young friend, couldn't wait to bandy the news around.

Beside her she heard the other woman's awkward little laugh before, put firmly in her place, she moved quickly out of Alex's sphere. And then, over the animated conversations and the light breeze, which brought with it the aroma of barbecued food and the intoxicating perfume of honeysuckle, she heard York's deeply drawled, 'Well handled, Mrs Masterton. Cynthia Pimm always was too damn nosy for her own good.'

'Careful, York.' From beneath her lashes Alex sent a guarded glance to where he was standing near the sighing hedge of rhododendrons which, only a few weeks ago, had been bright with crimson trumpets. 'You might find yourself in danger of slipping onto the side of the enemy.'

He laughed very softly, the sound carried over to her with the scents and sounds of the summer night.

'In that case we'd both be traitors, wouldn't we, my love?' he whispered, and though she knew his endearment was anything but loving it nevertheless sent a reckless little leap of hope along her veins.

They were on the perimeter of the lawn, below the steps that cut through the rhododendrons to the wilder stretches of the garden, just the two of them now, host and hostess snatching a few moments' guarded privacy. Or that was what it must look like to anyone watching, Alex thought distractedly, a long sigh escaping her at the pain caused by York's continuing suspicions.

'I'm only a traitor in so far as I allow myself to stay here and take your accusations,' she breathed, feeling the throb of tension in her pulse as he took a few silent strides towards her.

'Why do you, Alexia?'

Her eyes widened as she met his probing gaze with wounded bewilderment. Hadn't he initially ordered her to stay? What was he saying? That he didn't want her there any more? That he'd grown tired of all this pretence . . . ?

Oh, darling, don't!, she pleaded silently.

'I'll tell you why.' His voice rasped thickly across the shadowy yet impregnable barrier between them. 'Because you can't tear yourself away. You're as much a prisoner as I am beneath this charade of lies and marital civility, dearest. But inside each of us there's something fierce and consuming—more consuming—' his chin jerked roughly upwards '—than even that blaze up there.'

An animated turn in the party's conversation made them both look up in the direction he had indicated. Flames were rising from both sides of the gorseland now, leaping upwards on two distinct paths of fire.

'I've never seen a blaze like it.'

'Do you think it will reach the valley?'

'If it does, then those houses had better watch out!'

A wave of exaggerated speculation spread through the party. Most of the guests were now standing on the terrace, or on the nearside edge of the lawn for a better view.

'It's amazing how the human animal is totally fascinated by the vagaries of nature,' York commented drily at her shoulder. 'Fire. Flood. Eruption.'

'It's probably the power of it that excites,' she said, relieved to be on safer ground with him now. 'I find it scary.'

'Do you?' He laughed—a tight, sceptical sound. 'Are you saying you've never been excited by something you can't control, Alexia?'

She touched her tongue to her lips as she met that disturbingly beautiful gaze. He knew she had been by him. That was what his words were deliberately serving to remind her.

'It's so long ago,' she said brittly. 'I really don't remember.'

'Is that a challenge, darling?' He clicked his tongue in mocking disapproval. 'Because, if so, then the way you look tonight...' With heart-stopping precision he made a slow, studied appraisal of her swept-up hair, her pale throat and shoulders, the alluring scarlet of her dress. 'It could prove an irresistible one to any man.'

The tension that had started in her veins now crept insidiously along her spine. 'But you aren't any man, are you, York?'

'No,' he said quietly, slipping a hand into the pocket of his trousers. 'I'm your husband. And there isn't any man here who doesn't envy me tonight.'

Alex's throat tightened, eyes drawn unwittingly to the expanse of white shirt that his action had revealed. She uttered a tense little laugh. 'Why on earth would they envy you?'

'Why?' His smile was almost self-derisive. 'Because they know I can't look at you without being a slave to my own physical responses, darling. Because they think all I have to do is take you to bed to make my wildest fantasies come true.'

Alex's senses seemed to cease functioning. 'But they don't know, do they?' Her throat was dry, her heart beating for all it was worth.

'What? That I'd only have to touch you now to know that you'd respond to me. That I could satisfy every one of those...fantasies...if only I were weak—or foolish— enough to be tempted.'

'Like Adam?' Her voice was a mere squeak. 'Blameless for wanting the apple?'

'Except that I wouldn't be blameless, would I, darling? I'd be as guilty as hell and wallow in my own unpardonable downfall.'

Alex felt her breasts swell and tighten painfully beneath the soft fabric of her dress, felt the throb of primitive need stir way down in her loins.

If he had been drinking steadily all evening, like most of the other men, she might have expected him to be talking like this, but he hadn't. He was stone-cold sober, and it was that knowledge that sent fear, with a whole host of reckless impulses, spiralling through her blood.

The fire was out of hand now: two leaping giants of crimson sending showers of angry sparks into the air, a pair of rivals, hell-bent on destruction, moving relentlessly up the tinder-dry hillside, which, as everyone stood mesmerised, suddenly joined to create one gigantic inferno that produced an almighty, awe-inspired gasp from most of those watching.

Alex shuddered, turning away, and was glad when Ron and Debbie came up to join them again, relieving her of the tension caused by that unsettling conversation with York.

After that her time seemed to be monopolised by guests—people to whom she had only spoken at the start of the evening, some of whom had been at the wedding, others who hadn't, but all of whom were interested in knowing more about this curiously silver-haired young woman who had whisked the dynamic York Masterton into a swift and surprising marriage.

It was an effort to keep smiling, to pretend to everyone that everything between her and the charismatic man standing beside her was as it should be, and as the evening wore on it became more and more of a strain.

Above the town, the fire was dying down, at last brought under control, probably by the joint efforts of the local Fire Service and the National Parks Department as, so she remembered York telling her during the evening, much of the scenic countryside surrounding them was held in trust for the nation.

Gradually, too, the guests started to trickle away— save for Kay and a few others, Alex noticed as she came out of the house from seeing Ron and Debbie off and saw the small group on the terrace engaged in a pre-parting conversation with York.

He looked as fresh and elegant as he had at the start of the evening, she couldn't help thinking reluctantly, while she felt spent and drained with the exertion of pre-tending, even without the natural fatigue of early pregnancy.

'Why don't you go up? I'll take care of things here.'

Had he realised how weary she was? Alex wondered, feeling the burn of his dark interest, contemplative, flint-hard. Or was he merely playing the caring bridegroom still, for the sake of the others?

Nevertheless, she bade the remaining guests good-night and, grateful to York for suggesting it, slipped away to her room.

It was warm in the bedroom and she went over to the window and flung it wide open. The little group she'd left were still there and so engrossed in conversation that they didn't hear her. York was saying something that made everyone laugh, the sound of Kay's laughter echoing prettily above everyone else's. Then York glanced up, his attention turned fully towards Alex. She swallowed, smiled uneasily, though it was too dark for him to notice, and shrank swiftly away into the shadows.

He probably wouldn't be up for hours yet, she thought, wondering if, when the others left, he would ask Kay to stay.

A small sound left her lips as the thought acted like heat on a raw burn.

Dear God, how could she bear it? She battled to re-strain a sob, tortured by images of the other woman locked in her husband's arms, bringing her emotions

under control with an agonising tightening of her throat
as she fumbled with the back zip of her dress.

It stuck and she groaned wretchedly, tried to tug it
down and only succeeded in locking it deeper into the
fabric.

'Oh, hell!'

A shaft of light fell across one wall.

'Undressing in the dark, Alexia?'

The door had opened so quietly that she had failed
to hear it and she spun round as though on a
pivot.

'York!'

'Why so surprised? This was my bedroom,' he reminded her in a partly mocking, partly admonishing
voice.

'How come you remembered?' she taunted brittly,
noticing that somewhere between here and the terrace
he had discarded his jacket. 'Did your girlfriend suddenly decide she needed her beauty sleep?'

He didn't answer. She didn't think he would, so,
hurting, she was compelled to go on, 'Did she keep up
appearances better than I would have done when you
took her to that fête the other day?'

His breath seemed to rasp thickly through his lungs.
'She was organising the gymkhana—you know that. It
seemed sensible not to bother taking two cars. What were
you doing? Keeping tabs on me?' he queried, sounding
half-amused now, guessing, of course, that she had seen
them from the window.

'Well, since you're here,' she said, discomfited,
throwing caution to the winds, 'can you help me?' Her
heartbeat quickened as she saw him close the door.

He didn't need to ask what the difficulty was. The
lamps on the terrace threw a small pool of light over the
area of carpet on which she was standing.

'Stand still,' he ordered when she tried to avert her head and shoulders from his devastating proximity. His touch was electrifying, his fingers warm and sure against her flesh as they dealt swiftly and deftly with the refractory zip.

'While we're on the subject of beauty sleep, haven't you rather been overdoing it tonight—staying up so late? You're usually in bed by ten-thirty.'

'That isn't for vanity's sake,' she uttered as he tested the effortlessly freed zip.

'No, I would hope it's for the well-being of... your baby,' he said, that briefest of hesitations cutting her to the core.

'*My* baby?' She swung round, clutching the dress that was gaping fully at the back. '*Our* baby.' Her voice shook with emotion—with the effort of trying to convince him. And more emphatically she added, 'It's your baby too, York.'

Something fierce and darkly challenging leaped in his eyes. Those hard hands on her shoulders threatened to push her away and those strong masculine features, slashed with shadows from the terrace lamps, were contorted with an emotion she couldn't define. But then roughly—so roughly that she let out a small cry—he pulled her against him, stifling her murmur of protest as his mouth clamped hard over hers.

Everything else was forgotten in the consuming hunger of that kiss as desire fed desire, driving them both mindless with the uncontrolled and compelling urge for them to lose themselves in each other.

Differences didn't matter, suspicion and doubt and antagonism all melting in the inferno of need that possessed each of them as unbearably as it did the other.

'God, I want you!'

York's breathless declaration was torn from the soul, shuddering from him, as urgently he tugged at the dress he'd just freed so that it fell away from her, slipping to the floor. His hands followed the same path, travelling down her ribcage, over her smooth hips, cupping her buttocks to press her lower body against the grinding hardness of his.

Standing only in her lacy briefs and flat sandals, she felt the heat of his hands beneath her buttocks, the sensuous silk of his shirt seeming to burn against the excruciating sensitivity of her breasts.

'You have the loveliest body I've ever held in my arms. A man could go insane...'

There was anger in his own need for her. She could sense it in the raw quality of his voice. But she was the one going insane! With wanting him so much! she thought, a sob rising in her throat as his hands slid upwards over her ribcage again to close over the creamy luxury of her breasts.

'Oh, York, I can't...' What was she trying to say? That she was so on fire for him she couldn't take too much of this...?

'It's too late for that, darling.' He'd misunderstood her. Hopelessly she realised it as he swept her up into his arms, carried her over to the bed. 'Tonight there'll be no separate rooms, no driving me crazy with imagining you lying here while I go mad lying somewhere else, burning up with the knowledge of what hell is like not to have you. Tonight, my love, you're going to show your husband just what paradise really means!'

She trembled at the arousing determination of his promise, one coherent thought surfacing above her reeling senses—that Kay couldn't have told him. Perhaps the woman hadn't seen her with Lonnie Burrowes, because she couldn't believe it was Kay's integrity that had stopped her from informing York. She only knew that tonight this man was hers, that he wanted to be with her—this man whom she loved with the proof of the new life that was growing inside her, this man whom she loved so much that it hurt.

A sob shuddered through her from the acceptance that she would always love him, sensation piling upon sensation as his weight came down on hers, crushing her slender frame beneath the hard domination of his.

From the urgency of his lips and hands and the grinding pressure of his body, she thought he would take her there and then, and would have been ready for him had he chosen to, only he didn't. He didn't even undress at first.

From the soft silver of her hair, which he had loosened, down over her throat and breasts to the as yet only slight thickening of her waist, he watched her body flower and blossom as he caressed it with a mind-blowing, consummate skill.

She couldn't take it, and yet she wanted more—for there to be nothing else but this heaven and the way York was worshipping her body.

Those warm hands were removing the last scrap of lace from her body, caressing the smooth roundedness of her hips, her thighs, the slim, shapely length of her legs. She could hear the ragged quality of his breathing, and gloried in the knowledge that the very scent of her excited him as he inhaled the erotic perfume of her skin.

'Alexia.' His thumbs gently stroked her feet. She could feel each of his warm palms under her sensitive insteps as he breathed her name, his lips against the vivid red tips of her toes.

Shadows chased across the darkened room from the lamps still burning above the terrace, sparse patches of light falling across her body, illuminating her soft curves as they illuminated York's dark, sombre features. He was looking down at her with an intensity of desire that took her breath away, but something as deep and dark as pain showed beneath the enviable thickness of his lashes.

She was too much a prisoner of her own desire to give much thought to it then, as slowly he drew her feet apart, his hands moving with unbelievable sensuality along the smooth length of her legs.

Erotic had only been a word until then—until he drove her into a sobbing delirium as he tasted the sweet nectar of her body.

'Oh, York...don't make me wait any more. Don't torture me like this!' She was pleading with him now, but she didn't care, not even that he might taunt her with her own desire at some time in the future.

She only knew she wanted him—here and now—inside her; she wanted to welcome the father of her baby into the secret pathway to her womb, wrap her legs around him so that he would never leave her again, tell him how much she loved him, hear him breathing from the depths of his soul how much he loved and needed her.

But she remained silent on that score and so did he, although, as if her silent desire had conveyed the intensity of her need to him, he breathed hoarsely, 'Do you think you're the only one who's hurting?'

For a moment, as he drew away, she thought he was going to abandon her, leave her in torturous frustration because of that pain she could see in his eyes, but it was only to remove the clothes she had been clawing at in her wild desire.

And then he was sliding into her, granting the only thing that mattered, first with an initial restraint which she realised was concern for their unborn child, then with a driving energy as he finally lost control.

'*Alexia.*' If a word could convey all his feelings, that was it. His breath shuddered through him as he took them both over the brink of ecstasy into the paradise he had demanded from her earlier, but which was theirs to share now, a total union of two hearts, two minds, two bodies, so that eventually they fell asleep, their hunger slaked at last, fulfilled in each other's arms.

CHAPTER TEN

WHEN Alex awoke the next morning she was alone.

After showering and teaming a cool beige wrap-around skirt with a white sleeveless cotton blouse, she came light-heartedly into the dining room expecting to see York, but saw only Joyce clearing his used breakfast dishes from the table.

'He went out early,' the housekeeper informed her when she asked. 'He had a phone call and went out in a rush. I expect he didn't want to disturb you.'

'But it's Sunday,' Alex murmured, mainly to herself. She shrugged. 'Never marry a workaholic,' she said wryly, instantly regretting the remark as she recalled Celia's telling her once that Joyce's young husband had been an unemployed and hopeless gambler before the woman had had enough and finally divorced him, from then on devoting all her time to the Masterton men.

Feeling ravenous this morning, though, Alex readily took up the housekeeper's offer of a substantial breakfast, and smiled when the woman crooned satis-factorily over her empty plate.

'It's good to see you've got your appetite back again,' she commented, and with her usually austere features softening she added, 'They say it gets easier after the first three months.'

Alex made some appropriate, amiable response, unable to tell Joyce that it had been more than just her pregnancy that had been robbing her of her appetite over the past few weeks. She wondered, though, as she had been wondering since that day when York had come back and discovered Lonnie in the house, what interpretation

the woman must have placed on York's spending so much
time in London, on the separate rooms they occupied
here whenever he chose to stay.

But now it would be different, she vowed with a private
little smile, stretching her arms luxuriously above her
like a contented cat. Last night had marked a turning
point in their marriage and everything was going to be
all right. They could put the past behind them—all the
doubt and suspicion. And if he had still been harbouring any concerns last night when he had come to
her room, then he surely couldn't be harbouring any
now? Not after that wildly passionate night they had
spent together!

She got up from the table, her left thumb unconsciously twisting the flat gold band of her wedding ring.

Oh, she felt good this morning! she decided, with her
other hand coming to rest automatically on her as yet
unnoticeably expanding middle. She was gaining York's
trust at last, and they could start making plans for the
baby. Start planning for the future as they should have
been doing weeks ago.

In the meantime, she thought, feeling restless and
strangely perplexed that he should have gone off without
telling her after their passionate reconciliation the previous night, she decided to kill time by taking herself
off for a drive in the Range Rover.

Perhaps it was inevitable, she thought later, that she
found herself taking that familiar turning out of town
towards the moor.

She didn't even need to step out of the vehicle to see
the dismal scene last night's fire had made of the hillside.
Everywhere she looked, over a vast area, was blackened
heath and bracken. In places, charred tree stumps lay in
sad testimony to the previous night's spectacular inferno, while here and there huge dark puddles remained
to remind her of the firefighters' grim task to control
the blaze.

A hawk lay on the air, hovering for a while, hoping for the chance of some hopelessly exposed, homeless creature amongst the devastation.

Like a vulture, she thought, with a little shudder as it gave up and after a moment soared away, leaving Alex following in its wake along the path she and York had taken that afternoon he had proposed.

She should have known it would be too much to hope for. Even so, when she saw only the still smouldering remains of what had once been the forester's hut, which, after the blissful happiness she had known here, she had affectionately thought of as *their* ruin, a lump came into her throat. The derelict little hut was now no more than a heap of sodden charcoal.

Understandably saddened, she turned back towards the Range Rover. What was it York had said that day—that the heather seed was stimulated by fire?

As I am by him, she thought, feeling suddenly as inexplicably vulnerable as that small, devastated shrub. But it needed to be burnt to promote new growth. Wasn't that what he had said? Even though last night's fire had been unintentional. So it would all grow again, she assured herself as she climbed back into the car. Just like the love between her and York...

Her pulses throbbed into life as she recalled the fierce heat of their passion the previous night. They might have been through a lot of unnecessary pain in living separate lives during the past few weeks, but now he had obviously accepted that she wasn't involved with Lonnie...

Impatient to see him again, she was in danger of exceeding the speed limit as she brought the car up the hill towards the house, and her heart swelled, excitement turning to a wild exhilaration when she came into the drive and saw his BMW slewed across the cobbles of the forecourt. It looked as though he had come back in a hell of a hurry.

Pulse racing, Alex threw her door closed and tripped lightly through the house, peering into each room, but he wasn't anywhere downstairs.

Face flushed, her hair tousled from her walk, she ran upstairs, striving to contain at least some of her joy at finding him home.

The door to his room was open and she raced breathlessly towards it, only to stop dead when she saw him tossing shirts and trousers, a folded suit and socks haphazardly into the suitcase lying open on the bed.

'What are you doing?' Her hand at her throat, Alex already knew the answer. He might have been packing in response to an urgent business call, but she could tell from the thunderous look on his face that that wasn't the case.

'What does it look like I'm doing?' He didn't even glance up. His casually clad leanness as he stooped to pick up a tie he had dropped displayed nothing but that familiar contempt.

'Why?' she whispered, coming into the room, unable to comprehend this sudden change in his mood. Unless...

He paused to glance up then, and his eyes were like chips of green ice.

'You really know how to play a man for a fool, don't you?' he said in a lethal whisper, tossing a folded sweater into the case. 'You almost convinced me last night with that oh, so sweet mouth and the eagerness of that sexy, irresistible body. But, much as I appreciate your readiness to accommodate me in your bed, darling, I prefer a wife without too many divided loyalties!'

The excited flush had faded from Alex's cheeks. 'What do you mean?' she queried. As if she didn't know! 'Kay!'

Involuntarily, the name slipped through her lips—an indictment, she realised despairingly from the cold, accusing tilt of his head.

'If you didn't want me to find out you were still carrying on with Burrowes you really should have been more careful, sweetheart.' The endearment was as scathing as it was meaningless.

So Kay had told him. But not last night at the party for some reason. Maybe she hadn't been able to catch him on his own. Or perhaps she had felt shunned when he had let her go home, along with the others, impatient as he must have appeared to be to spend the night with his wife. But she had made sure she let him know eventually about seeing her, Alex, in London. Perhaps she felt she owed it to him, without a thought—or perhaps she had thought, Alex considered bitterly—for the damage it would cause to his marriage.

'There's never been anything between us, York.' She had to let him know, try and make him understand. 'I went up to see him to try and persuade him to tell you that.'

'Really?' A thick eyebrow lifted with wounding scepticism. 'Just as you were doing when I came home that day and caught you both undressed!'

Of course, it all came back to that.

'We weren't both undressed!' she tossed back in hot defiance. 'At least, he wasn't!'

'Bravo for him! So what was he doing? Measuring up for new wardrobes?'

'In a manner of speaking, yes.' She ignored his harsh, mirthless laugh. 'Looking for skeletons in the closets. You know what type of journalist he is! I gave him the most innocuous interview I could think of.'

'What? In your underwear? In your bedroom?'

Dear heaven! Why wouldn't he believe her? 'I've tried to tell you before. I was upstairs changing and he came up and caught me unawares.'

Roughly he threw closed the suitcase. 'So, like the dutiful lady of the house, you politely asked him to stay.'

Alex's shoulders slumped and there was a bone-deep weariness to her face as she watched him snap each clasp into place with a hard, ominous click. 'To give him a simple story about us and try and satisfy his lust for gossip seemed the only sensible way to get rid of him, that was all.'

'Only that wasn't all you satisfied!'

'Stop it!'

Her screamed command dragged his gaze from its swift assessment of the half-emptied wardrobe, those grey-green eyes tugging censoriously over the wild silver of her hair, the heated colour infiltrating her pale skin.

'Planning on throwing that at me, Alexia?' His voice was cool, remarkably controlled in comparison, drawing her attention to the flat dark hairbrush she'd snatched off the duvet and which only a shred of control had stopped her from hurling at him across the bed. 'I'm afraid it's a case of like mother, like daughter, darling.'

Cruelly, he was reminding her of that ugly scene when Shirley, in her sexual humiliation, had kept repeatedly lashing out at him and, ashamed, Alex let the brush fall. She wasn't like Shirley, she thought, even if he believed she was—as he emphasised even as he went on, 'Perhaps I should have followed my initial instincts and realised that before we came this far down the road. But, just for the record, why did you have to entertain giving him an interview at all? What *gossip* exactly were you afraid of?'

A vice seemed to tighten around Alex's heart. There was so much at stake. Her marriage. Perhaps the security of her child's future. Yet his inexorable opinion of her—an opinion, she realised now, he had never really lost—locked her in paralysing silence. She'd die before she told him, or anyone, ever again.

He swore quietly under his breath when she failed to respond. 'What do you take me for, Alexia? A blind-headed fool? Sounds to me like the most convenient excuse for infidelity I've ever heard in my life! Oh, original, I'll grant you! But then you take top marks for originality, don't you, dearest?'

He moved around the bed, a predatory animal of hard, lean strength, his sensual taunt brutally bringing to mind something he had said when she had been learning to please him, weeks ago, in the heady days of their honeymoon.

'Don't touch me!' She recoiled from the brush of his hand against her cheek, aching for him to hold her, yet knowing she would only be surrendering to his need to hurt her if he did.

'Quite a turnabout from last night, isn't it?' he taunted, his flaying contempt stripping her to the core. 'What's the matter? Regretting being unfaithful to Burrowes? Does it really touch your conscience having two lovers at the same time? Because if it does then at least remember that *I'm* still your husband—the man you swore to honour as such!'

A raw ache started gnawing at Alex's heart. She could never convince him, not when he had made up his mind in such complete judgement against her.

'Those vows were mutual, York,' she uttered desolately. 'If you refuse to believe I'm telling the truth about this—what will be next? If you can't trust me enough to accept a thing I say then that's your problem, not mine.'

With a tug of heart-wrenching regret she saw that deep chest expand heavily. There was a long silence. Then, reaching for his case, his mouth pulling tightly, he said, 'Yes, darling. It seems that it is.'

She couldn't believe that she was allowing this to happen.

York! As she watched him stride out of the door, she wanted to run after him, call out to him, beg him to come back. Perhaps if she had told him the truth he might have stayed, but she didn't think so. If she had been able to in the beginning perhaps he might have thought differently, but she knew now that it was too late. What they were talking about was trust, and he had so convinced himself that she was like Shirley, whom he had never stopped despising for the way she had treated his uncle, that she doubted if anything would ever change his mind.

Last night he had wanted to believe her, she realised, tears stinging her eyes as she remembered the way he had made love to her—with a desperation that could only come from a man in love. But he was like Page, she thought desolately, so blinded by emotion that he couldn't see what his love was destroying. Shirley had been pregnant too, just like she was, she thought with an anguished sob of irony, when her father's dogmatism and stubbornness had driven her out of this house. And now the same thing was happening again...

'Oh, York, can't you *see*?' She said it aloud, a futile whisper, lost beneath the purposeful sound of the BMW starting up. She thought of the way she had driven in earlier, of her excitement at seeing his car there when she had come back from the moor, and it took all her strength not to break down entirely as she saw now that desolate scene up there this morning for exactly what it was—the destruction of all her foolish hopes and dreams when she had married York, and which, for a short period today, she had foolishly dared hope she could retrieve again. But she knew now, just as with the derelict little hut before the fire, that their marriage was already too far gone to rebuild.

Over the ensuing weeks things didn't improve between her and York. Some weekends he didn't even return, and if he did he barely spoke to her. And yet, despite the fact that he had transferred most of his personal effects to his London flat, that steel strength of integrity that was an inherent part of his character wouldn't allow him to abandon her altogether.

Despite his continuing refusal to listen on the occasions when she tried in vain to convince him that she wasn't having an affair with Lonnie, he still couldn't rule out that the child she was carrying was his. No offspring of his, he had made clear to her, would be deprived of its natural father, and to that end his raging sense of correctness made sure that Alex was adequately cared for as her pregnancy advanced.

It was like living with a stranger whenever he did decide to stay—a stranger she loved and needed more than she had ever loved and needed anyone in her life. And, although she couldn't have found fault with the physical comforts that he seemed determined to provide, he gave nothing of the one thing she desperately wanted from him—the warmth of his love—never guessing at what his cold remoteness was doing to her.

Though she didn't allow her loss of appetite to stop her eating regularly, which she was determined to force herself to do for the sake of her baby, she lost more and more sleep, and when she did manage to doze off her rest was plagued by vivid and tormented dreams.

The dreams were varied but they always ended in the same way. She was standing on the hill overlooking the town and little flames were licking through the grass under her feet. She was hopping and jumping to avoid them, but they were all around her, and when at last she managed to find a safe clearing her way was blocked by two huge flames ahead on either side of the path.

She could feel no warmth, no imminent danger, only their cold, blinding brilliance that had her shielding her eyes with an arm, crying out to them to let her through because somehow she knew that they were York and her grandfather. But when she looked back they had merged and become one, the more dominant consuming the other so that its brilliance was harsher, colder, and she knew then that there was only York.

Then she would awake sobbing, his name on her lips— an anguished plea in the darkness—and all she could do was to lay her hand against her swollen middle and find her solace in feeling his baby kick.

Celia came over for a few days during November, and York was compelled to remain at Moorlands for the duration of his mother's stay.

During that time he treated Alex with a restrained politeness that was almost impossible to bear, and she could tell, from the way she caught her mother-in-law studying them when the woman thought they weren't looking, that she knew something wasn't quite right.

'I did try to put her off,' York had told her coolly when he'd first announced that his mother was coming, 'but short of telling her the truth I didn't see what else I could sensibly do.'

'And what is the truth, York?' she had said, challenging him, her pale chignon and softly pregnant figure portraying a stark vulnerability against the potency of his hard, dark strength. 'That her son's so pigheaded that he can't see when he's making the biggest mistake of his life?'

But all he had said was, 'No, darling, not any more,' in an implacable tone that had somehow been at variance with the stretched bleakness of his features.

So Celia had come to stay, bright and brisk and more than ready to talk about her forthcoming grandchild and to accompany Alex shopping for the things she was going to need when the baby eventually came. And if her mother-in-law suspected that her son and his new wife were having teething problems then an inborn decorum prevented her from any tactless probing.

Joyce too—more than anyone, Alex thought—would have been aware of the continuing deterioration of her marriage, but she knew the housekeeper would never consider it her place to enquire into her employers' affairs, and even less divulge them to anyone outside—

although what anyone else thought Alex was too unhappy to care.

If York hadn't hated her mother quite so much, hadn't
incorrectly bracketed them together as deceitful and...

She couldn't even acknowledge the truth of what he
thought about her, admit it to herself. It was too horrid,
too nauseating, she thought with a sickening little
shudder that bitterly cold December day when things
finally came to a head. But if he hadn't likened her to
Shirley then perhaps it might have been different.
Perhaps then she might have been able to tell him...

She put a brake on her runaway thoughts as she let
herself into the house after driving back from Christmas
shopping in town. What was the point of thinking what
might have been?

The house was warm and welcoming as she came into
the hall. Joyce had already lit a fire in the lounge. She
recognised the distinctively sweet smell of smouldering
cherry wood from the tree Edmundo had taken down in
the orchard back in the summer.

Pulling off her gloves and tossing them onto the small
round polished table beside which she had discarded her
bags, she was just unfastening her thick creamy wool
jacket when a vehicle's headlights flashed through the
darkening afternoon, across the small leaded panes of
the hall window.

Alex opened the front door as Ron's dark, dusty
saloon screeched to a halt on the cobbles. He leapt out,
leaving the car door gaping, the headlights still glaring
through the dusk, and she knew even before she noticed
the tense lines of his face that this was no social call.

'Oh, Alexia! I've just come from the quarry!' He
sounded distraught, beside himself.

'What is it? What's wrong?' she pressed, baffled.

'York...'

She frowned as he came into the porch. 'York's in
London. If you want to come in—'

'No.' He was shaking his head. 'There's been an accident! He's not in London. He came to the quarry! He was driving down and one of the lorries...' He paused, breathing hard, while Alex stared at him, speechless. 'I don't know. The driver... He had a blackout or something. I only heard the crash as it ran into the wall! And York's car. It ran into York's car—'

'Is he all right?'

'I don't know. They can't get to him. They're trying to move the lorry. The fire services are there now, trying to—'

'*No!*'

Ron glanced at the slender hand suddenly clutching her midriff. 'I'm sorry. I shouldn't have told you like that. You'd better go in and sit down for a minute. I've got to get back—'

'No!' He had turned to go, but Alex caught his arm. 'You've got to take me with you!'

'I don't know. I... It could take hours—and in your condition—'

'*Please*...' He looked about to refuse again, anxious to be off, but her fingers locked like talons onto the thick sleeve of his donkey jacket. 'You've got to!'

He knew it was pointless arguing with her and in seconds they were speeding back down the drive, taking the road and then the long, narrow lane to the quarry.

Ron had been right. There were fire engines and two ambulances standing by. In the now raw dark winter's afternoon, their ominous blue lights sent a shiver of fear through Alex. She could see the way the lorry had jack-knifed into the red rock, severely damaging the nearside of the cab, but the driver appeared to be unharmed. They were helping him out as she and Ron arrived, leading him to one of the waiting ambulances, but she couldn't see the BMW. It was hidden behind the wheels of the metal hulk.

'He'll be all right,' she heard one of the rescuers assure the driver who must have been desperate to know.

And then she heard another voice as she raced towards the other men who were trying to move the lorry. 'He'll be lucky if he gets out of this alive!'

'*No!*'

The man turned and saw her, tried to restrain her as she ran, like someone demented, screaming and hammering against the bruising steel of the lorry.

'York!' She was crying his name aloud, feeling helplessly inadequate, sobs tearing at her body. 'Oh, no, *York*! Oh, please . . .' She turned to one of the men, her features lined with desperation. 'Please . . . you've got to get him out!'

'We're doing all we can, lady.' The man looked harassed, in no mood to speak to her. 'For goodness' sake, get her out of here!' he ordered over his shoulder to one of his men. But it was Ron who was suddenly there, putting comforting arms around her.

'He's going to be all right, Alexia. Believe me. York's going to be all right. Now come inside for a while. It's biting out here.'

Like a sleepwalker she allowed him to lead her into the warmth of the Portakabin. He brought her a cup of hot, sweet tea which she couldn't remember drinking. She kept going back outside. She couldn't stay in there, not when her husband was lying there, buried under the great hulk of that lorry. Perhaps still conscious. Needing her . . .

She kept out of the way of the rescue workers, but eventually nothing could induce her to go back inside. Not even Ron.

'Alexia, please. Think of the baby.' He took one of her hands and rubbed it between the rough warmth of his own. 'You should have gloves on,' he chided hoarsely. 'Where are your gloves?'

Where were they? In a half-daze she remembered pulling them off what seemed like half a century ago. What had she done with them?

'Alexia?' Suddenly, Debbie was there beside her, slipping a plump, maternal arm around her waist. 'Ron's right. You should come away,' she advised with the gentle patience that had successfully raised four boisterous boys. 'It won't do any good standing here...just waiting.'

'I've got to,' Alex murmured, and silently added, He doesn't know I love him, and if I go inside now he might never know.

She had twinges in her stomach, too, that were verging on pains, and she felt decidedly uncomfortable, but right then that didn't seem important. All that mattered was to see York climb out of his car safe and unharmed. She knew his chances were slim, but as the rescue team started to tow the lorry free at last she found she was praying desperately for a miracle.

She didn't know how many hours had gone by since Ron had first come to tell her about the accident. Perhaps it was one or two—perhaps a dozen. But now, as the lorry was shifted forwards, under the extra lights that had been set up around the quarry to help the rescuers work the damage to the BMW became apparent.

Its back end was indescribably crushed where it had been forced into the wall, but the front offside wing and bonnet had sustained remarkably little damage, apart from a rather nasty crease in the driver's door. Unbelievably, Alex thought she saw a movement inside.

She rushed towards the car, but was restrained by one of the rescue workers who was keeping a small band of anxious quarrymen and other concerned onlookers from getting too close.

'He's my husband!' she stressed plaintively, but the man wouldn't let her pass.

'I'm sorry, Mrs Masterton, but it's best that you hold on a minute until we assess what condition he's in.'

'No!' she protested. 'It isn't your husband!' She tried to push her way forcefully past him but the man was determined not to let her and she didn't have the energy to put up too much resistance. She felt spent and weak, and her pains were getting worse.

Frantically, looking over the man's shoulder, she realised that the rescue team was having difficulty getting the car door open.

'Is he going to be all right?' Oh, dear heaven...

'Alex!' She didn't know how he'd got there, but suddenly Lonnie Burrowes was beside her. 'My God, you look dreadful!' She was only vaguely aware of his hand at her elbow, of hearing him assuring the other man that he would see she was all right.

'Let me go!' She tried to shrug off his restraining hold as the other man, glad, no doubt, to be relieved of what he must have considered to be a near-hysterical wife, was striding off to attend to more pressing matters elsewhere.

She glared at Lonnie when he refused to grant her request, demanding, 'How did you get in here anyway? This is private land. The Press haven't been allowed in here.'

'I'm not the Press. I'm a friend of yours, aren't I? That's what I told the man at the entrance, otherwise they'd never have let me in.'

'A friend of mine!' Alex struggled in his grasp. 'You've never been a friend of mine! Not now! Not ever!'

'Oh, come on, Alex...you're overwrought, and it's understandable. But you might find yourself needing a friend if...if York...well, if he...'

'If I do what, Burrowes? Kick the bucket?'

Alex spun round, pulled by the familiarly deep voice which for hours she had been wondering if she would ever hear again.

'York!' She was unable to believe what she was seeing.

He was out of the car, leaning heavily against the buckled wing. Jacketless, he looked tired and dishevelled, his usually immaculate shirt crumpled, his black hair falling untidily across his forehead, and there was an ugly gash above his right eye, but he was alive!

'Sorry to disappoint you if that's what you were hoping, old chap,' he drawled sarcastically, still in control, despite his ordeal, as he looked venomously at Lonnie. 'And unless you want a broken nose—get your hands off my wife!'

'York!' As Lonnie obeyed the intimidating command, Alex rushed forward, somehow, amazingly, stopping short of allowing herself to run into his arms. He wouldn't welcome it. Besides, one of the ambulancemen had come up to him, was suggesting he go with them to the hospital for a check-up, saying something about York having been concussed.

'I'm perfectly all right.'

'Nevertheless, I feel you should let the doctor look at you, sir—'

'I said I'm all right!'

The authority in that deep voice was sufficient for the other man to realise it was pointless arguing, but Alex was determined not to be bullied by him as the ambulanceman moved away.

'You really ought to,' she whispered, worried for him more than for herself, although she was beginning to feel decidedly unwell. 'You might feel all right, but you...well...you might not be.'

A fleeting smile lifted one corner of his mouth. 'And would you worry if I wasn't?'

Against the backdrop of activity, of revving engines and shouted commands, for a moment, it seemed, they were entirely alone.

'Of course I would,' she choked, wondering if she had imagined that odd inflexion in his voice. 'You don't know what I've been through...'

'Don't I?' His eyes were dark, fathomless pools of concealed emotion. 'I must say your concern surprises

me. A man could die for just half of it.' That raw intensity was still there behind the hard façade. But was
he being sarcastic, hurting her when he had to be able
to see the anxiety in her face, that she had been out of
her mind with worry? But he wasn't looking at her now.
He was looking at Lonnie. Lonnie, whom she had forgotten. 'And what were you doing, Burrowes? Mopping
up her tears?' His tone, distinctly threatening, made
Lonnie visibly recoil.

'I—I thought she didn't look well.' He sounded un-
customarily nervous, not looking too good himself at
that moment. 'I thought she was going to faint or
something.'

'Did you?' York's expression was hard, inscrutable,
although there was a dark question in the grey-green eyes
that rested on Alex. 'If she were then I think that would
be my concern, Burrowes—not yours.' Her insides, which
seemed to have been wrenched out of her with all the
emotion she had expended over the course of the evening,
now lurched with the depth of her feelings for York as
his arm came around her waist. 'What are you doing
here anyway? I hadn't imagined this to be a free-for-all
for the Press.'

Lonnie looked up challengingly now into York's
strong, commanding features. 'I was in Taunton doing
a story. Rang the office and was told to get down here
as fast as I could. It was on the local news.'

'What were you hoping for? A first-rate tragedy to
publish in that rag of yours?' York suggested roughly.
'Well, as I said, sorry to disappoint you, but I'm not
dead yet, so you're going to have to go back empty-
handed. You're not welcome here, Burrowes. You or
your type of journalism. So get out of here now and
don't ever let me see you lay a finger on my wife again!'

She could feel the tautening of that strong arm across
her back, the almost protective hand that lay against her
middle. She couldn't understand why he was being so

possessive. Her heart was rejoicing even as her mind was telling her that he was only acting with atavistic aggression, as any male animal would, asserting what he believed were his rights over a rival male.

'Don't worry.' Lonnie made a cynical sound down his nose. 'I've never touched your wife and I wouldn't—even with a bargepole.' His sneering glance over her held all the resentment she knew sprang solely from bruised male pride, from her refusal to go out with him all those years before. 'I'm afraid I'd have to be really hard up—even desperate—before I'd stoop to shacking up with someone whose mother was a hooker!'

The lights in the quarry illuminated the shock on York's face, the satisfaction on Lonnie's, and Alex pressed her lids tight against the sight of both of them, against the agony of truth she had been carrying with her since she was eighteen.

'Get off my land!' She heard York's intimidating whisper, saw how he seemed to snarl as he took one swift, threatening stride towards the other man. 'Get out of here right now—and if you dare to print one word of that I'll have your paper in court so fast you and your editor won't know what's hit you. Is that clear?'

He was already speaking to Lonnie's back; it was almost laughable the way the journalist was scurrying away, except that Alex didn't feel like laughing. Her joy that York was unharmed, that he seemed for some reason to have forgotten how much he distrusted her was overshadowed by the shame and guilt and the sullied feeling she had known for the past ten years.

'Is it true?' His face was lined with disbelief—with repugnance—as he looked down at her, guessed. Even so he turned her roughly to face him. 'Is it?'

Tears stung her eyes, but she struggled to control them. 'Oh, York, not now.' She sagged wearily against him. She just wanted him to hold her.

More gently now, though, he lifted her chin with his forefinger.

'Tell me, Alexia.' His voice too was unexpectedly gentle. 'What did he mean?'

Beneath the thick coat, Alex's shoulders lifted as she took a deep breath. 'I told him—a long time ago—when I was in New Zealand. I had to. I couldn't bear it, you see. When I came home that afternoon from college and surprised her—surprised them both—found out what she was doing—she just got angry with me at first—said it was all my fault, that she wouldn't have been in that situation if it hadn't been for me. But then she cried and said she'd had to earn more money somehow—that she was doing it for me. She said there were only a couple of regulars—and I think there were. But they paid her!'

Her hands flew to her face. 'Oh, God! I hated it! After she died and I went to New Zealand, I just couldn't forget it. I felt dirty—as if it was me. I told Lonnie because he seemed like a friend. I thought I could trust him. I found out quickly enough what he could be like but it was too late then. I just never imagined that he'd move back to England—let alone try and use the knowledge against me at the first available chance.'

Through the glare of the lights and the commotion still going on behind them, she saw understanding dawning in York's face.

'Is that why you let him into our bedroom, felt you had to offer him some story to keep him from writing gossip? Was he threatening to print it? Is that it, Alexia? Is that the hold he's had over you all these months?'

She closed her eyes against the dark intensity of his, nodding her head.

'Why didn't you tell me?' His voice sounded incredulous. 'Why didn't you let me sort him out? Why were you prepared to sacrifice our marriage rather than tell me the truth?'

Her head dropped against his shoulder, covered by the jacket one of the rescuers had placed around it. He made her feel so wonderfully warm and safe...

'I don't know, I—I couldn't—and I knew you hated Shirley—so much. I couldn't bear to hear you saying things about her. Knowing what she...was...hurt enough without giving you another weapon to verbally destroy her with. And whatever else she was—bitter—unforgiving—selfish, even—she was still my mother. I guess she needed money because she was drinking so heavily. It became such a problem with her in the end.

'I know she only sank so low in direct rebellion against my grandfather, but even so she did her best for me, and, though you might not find this easy to believe, through all her mixed-up life she never really loved or cared for any man but my father...except perhaps for...' She didn't need to spell it out. He knew the devastating yet unintended affect he himself had had on his older cousin.

'We can all be blind,' he said quietly. 'I dare say my uncle was partly if not as much to blame as Shirley.' And when Alex looked at him, surprised, he went on, 'Oh, I know he could be a tyrant! Half-tyrant, half-floundering parent trying to hang onto the person he loved most and going the wrong way about it.

'I know that now,' he breathed. 'I also know I'm like him in many ways. Until I experienced at first hand how a man could go half out of his mind with jealousy—possessiveness—I wouldn't have believed it. Love can be destructive as well as beautiful—that's one thing I've learned.' It was amazing what he was admitting to her then. 'Perhaps Page wouldn't yield once too often and Shirley just had no more to give by the time he realised it. Perhaps,' he suggested gently, 'she really wanted to come home and was just too proud.'

Alex lifted her face to his, her expression pained, yet hopeful. 'Do you really think so?'

He gave a self-deprecating grimace. 'It does rather run in the family—through the male and female line.'

She essayed a rather distracted smile. Something was happening to her and she wasn't sure what, but her pains were almost cramping now.

Unconsciously, she ran her hand over the back of her soft skirt beneath her jacket. She felt so uncomfortable...

'Pride destroyed them,' he said in a low voice. 'Don't let's allow it to happen to us, Alexia.'

Love shone in her eyes. How could she even have dreamed of letting it? Even so, she couldn't resist saying, 'You were the one who was too proud to yield!' And with a roll of her eyes she added, 'And over Lonnie!'

'Don't remind me of that.' He sounded and looked suddenly angry—not angry at her but at himself. 'I suppose I couldn't believe my luck when you said you'd marry me. I suppose I was looking for ulterior motives. And you must admit that seeing you with Burrowes that day and then afterwards hearing from Kay that she'd seen you with him provided one that I was too ready to accept.

'But you always responded to me when I touched you. I kept trying to convince myself that you'd be the same with any man—that it wasn't just me. But earlier, when I was trapped in that car, I heard you screaming. I seemed to be floating in and out of consciousness, but somehow I knew it wasn't a dream. I tried to open the door and then the window to try and tell you I was all right but they wouldn't open. And you kept screaming my name— as if you couldn't bear to imagine... As if you...'

His face was etched with lines of doubt, as though he couldn't quite believe what he was trying to say. She reached up to touch her fingers lightly to the dark bruising above the wound at his temple.

'Oh, my love...what did you think? That I didn't love you? I've always loved you. Since that first time you kissed me when I was seventeen. I thought I was depraved because of how I felt about you, because you were so angry. I even convinced myself I was, after I found out about...that I was like...well, you know. I couldn't let another man near me. I thought it was because I despised myself so much, but it wasn't only that. I didn't realise until I came back here—until you kissed me again that day in the Doone Valley—that really I'd just been waiting for you...'

There was a fresh smear on his cheek and she frowned at the bright, damp blood on her fingers, at the dark, jagged line where the blood had already coagulated around the wound above York's eye.

Something was wrong! She could feel it. There was blood on her hand, on her clothes. But it wasn't from him. It was hers!

'Oh, *no*...!'

She stared, paralysed, at her hand, although that small sob and the fear in her face had York instantly taking control.

She might have fainted if he hadn't caught her, using what strength he had to sustain her as he pulled her back with him against the BMW, supporting her with his knee, and through a swirling haze she heard his voice, urgent and commanding. 'For goodness' sake, get that ambulance over here!'

They were on their way. Sirens blaring, lights flashing. She could see the reflection of the ominous blue lamp even through the darkened glass.

York was beside her, his strong hand holding hers, telling her everything was going to be all right—only it wasn't.

Emotion squeezed out from between her closed lids. Perhaps they would think she was crying because of the pain. York loved her, and he knew now that she loved him. Things were going to be all right between them, and of course she was happy about that. But why was

she going to have to pay for that happiness with such a
cruel twist of fate?

She was just twenty-seven weeks pregnant and she was
losing her baby. The baby whose identity York had
doubted, just as he had doubted hers in the beginning,
and now—now that he was ready to accept it, accept
them both—it was too late.

CHAPTER ELEVEN

THE bright morning light played across the yellow of a vase of daffodils standing on the landing window-sill.

March already, Alex marvelled, bending to inhale their softly evocative scent. In a week or two spring would really be here. Yesterday they had gone for a walk, up there on the moor to the exact spot where York had proposed, and already new heather was springing up almost in defiance of the ravages of last summer's fire. It was a time for new hopes. A new beginning...

For the past two and a half months it had been just the two of them, without misunderstanding, without suspicion. With only tenderness and, later, a rekindling of passion and desire, and always that interminable understanding she had needed—especially during those early weeks—from York.

She knew he had blamed himself at first for what had happened, although the doctors had assured them that it would have happened anyway, that there had been physical factors involved which, as well as being life-threatening to Alex, would have prevented her from carrying her baby to its full term.

Sunlight spilled across the floor as she pushed open the door to the nursery. She had sat in here for long spells at a time at first, cuddling the tiny toys, fingering the bedding in the unused cot.

What was it Kay had said when she had bumped into her in town back in the winter? 'Well, at least you're young. If...' She had hesitated for a moment, looking embarrassed, but had nevertheless carried on insensitively to say, 'Well, you know...you can have other babies...'

Only she hadn't wanted others. She had wanted that one. Nicholas. That was what she had called him. Little Nicholas. Her first.

But now it was time to put the past and those traumatic memories behind her. Today was an important day. She shouldn't be spending it dwelling on unhappy thoughts.

'Well, Mrs Masterton...are you ready?'

She turned round swiftly as York came up behind her. He was casually dressed in a dark padded jacket and trousers, waiting for her, a discerning movement of his lips, as he noted where her interest lay, assuring her that he understood.

But did he? Could a man ever really know a mother's fierce love for the baby she'd carried for over six months, she wondered achingly—the desperation when it all started to go wrong and the anguish of being without that child?

There were fine lines permanently etched around his eyes that hadn't been there last summer, and now, as she noticed the tension in those otherwise strong, gaunt features, she thought, of course he did.

There were crocuses everywhere as they set out on their journey towards Taunton, the small, bright heads flecking verges and banks and gardens with purple, white and gold. Pink and yellow primulas and blue hyacinths filled pots alongside russet beds of wallflowers. One sprig of white plum blossom peeped bravely above a garden wall. And, high on the hill that rose to the blue sky above the town, young lambs gambolled beside the calmer, sedate figure of their mothers. The whole world, it seemed, was drunk with new life.

'How are you feeling?'

Alex glanced across the car to catch York's warm, sagacious smile.

'Nervous,' she admitted, knowing that with her hair drawn back into a soft bun, exposing her face to him, she couldn't pretend anything else. 'You?'

His lips moved in an expressively wry gesture, but he didn't say anything. He was about the most confident man she knew. He gave television interviews, conducted executive-level meetings, dealt with a lot of important people. Yet even he, she realised, surprised, was feeling jittery this morning.

'Do I look all right?' she asked much later as they were nearing their destination.

He laughed affectionately at her over-anxious question, glanced at her hands moving nervously over the skirt of her chic black and white check suit.

'More beautiful than I've ever seen you look before, darling.' He gave her a lazy, appreciative smile which, in spite of the importance of the day, sent a throb of familiar excitement through her blood. 'Don't worry,' he advised softly, and then with a teasing light in his eyes murmured, 'You're going to pass the interview with flying colours.'

Alex chewed on her bottom lip. 'I've already got the job,' she said quietly.

'And you're going to handle it like only you can,' he reassured her in a gentle, understanding voice as he brought the new BMW to a halt in the car park of the huge and rambling modern red-brick building.

'Just one thing...' A restraining hand was on her shoulder as she made to get out. He leaned over to take something out of the glove compartment. An eternity ring! she realised, when he opened the little box.

'What's this for?' Her eyes were shining like the circle of diamonds and deep sapphires he'd slipped onto her finger and now pressed up against the thin gold band of her wedding ring.

'That's just to say, I love you,' he whispered, bringing emotion surging through her as he dipped his head to press his lips to the finger he had just adorned.

'Oh, York . . .' She closed her eyes, the unique blend of her pale skin, dark lashes and soft silver hair giving her the appearance of a madonna—a madonna whose face was radiant with love. They hadn't bothered with an engagement ring, but this meant more—so much more.

She felt his lips brush the tip of her nose. 'Now go in there,' he murmured with a lift of his chin towards the building. 'And show the world what a wonderfully clever lady I married.'

She almost ran along the clean, scrubbed corridor, hurrying ahead of him though she knew he was right behind her. He would always be behind her, beside her, she thought joyfully, controlling her nerves as a door opened and the woman she recognised—knew on first-name terms now—came out of a small ante-room and smiled a good morning at her, before placing the squalling, white-shawled little body into her arms.

He had weighed less than two pounds when he had been delivered by Caesarean section that awful night in December—something the doctors had insisted on for her sake as well as the baby's. When she had woken up after the operation, she hadn't even opened her eyes before asking if he was all right. It had seemed like an age before they had told her, though it must have been just a matter of seconds—just two or three heartbeats when the whole word had seemed to hang in the balance—before someone had reassured her that her son was alive.

They had put a little tube in his nose to shoot that first, life-giving puff of air into his tiny lungs to start him breathing. And from then on he had done it all by himself, although technology had been on hand to assist him through the long, worrying period in an incubator.

Alex smiled down at his little puckered face. Amazingly, he had stopped crying as soon as she had taken him into her arms and was now making contented gurgling noises.

'Thank you.' She looked up with appreciative eyes, smiling at the sister. 'Thanks for everything.'

The woman, an understanding mother of three in her thirties, touched her hand.

'You did your bit as well—both of you.' Her rather nervous smile acknowledged the dynamism of the baby's father, that slight flush always there whenever she spoke to York. 'Supporting him. Putting out all those positive vibes to help him on his way. As for you, Alexia... If you hadn't been in every day feeding him, supplying all that nourishing milk for us to freeze...'

Her simple shrug said it all, but she was thinking what a perfect couple they made, and what a beautiful little baby they had created. He might still be only the size of some newborn infants, but by his first birthday he would have caught up. They usually did.

She walked with them to the end of the corridor.

'Bye, Nicholas,' she crooned, touching two fingers to his tiny head.

He instantly started to wail.

'He's got quite a pair of lungs on him,' York remarked drily.

'And quite a temper too, I believe,' said the sister, grinning.

'In that case he takes after his father,' Alex giggled, and caught the laughing challenge as she looked up into York's beautiful eyes. That scar under his right eyebrow, like the emotional scars of her past, was fading by the day.

'You'd better believe it,' he drawled as the woman left them to themselves, his remark sending a satisfied warmth through Alex.

So much suspicion, she reflected. So much doubt. And now he'd even admit to his own shortcomings just to hear people tell him his son was like him. That was fatherhood for you!

Perhaps at some stage, she thought, holding her baby close as she came out into the sunlight with York's arm around her, she might even try to trace her own father. But if she couldn't, what did it really matter? She had everything she could want—had ever wanted or ever would want. She had York. She had little Nicholas. She had a family.

MILLS & BOON®

Next Month's Romances

♡

Each month you can choose from a wide variety of romance novels from Mills & Boon. Below are the new titles to look out for next month from the Presents and Enchanted series.

Presents™

LONG NIGHT'S LOVING	Anne Mather
THE MARRIAGE WAR	Charlotte Lamb
TWO-WEEK WIFE	Miranda Lee
ACCIDENTAL NANNY	Lindsay Armstrong
HUSBAND BY CONTRACT	Helen Brooks
SOLUTION: SEDUCTION!	Elizabeth Oldfield
THE DADDY DEAL	Kathleen O'Brien
A MARRIED WOMAN?	Susanne McCarthy

Enchanted™

THE TROUBLE WITH TRENT!	Jessica Steele
A MARRIAGE HAS BEEN ARRANGED	Anne Weale
BABY, YOU'RE MINE!	Leigh Michaels
THE INNOCENT AND THE PLAYBOY	Sophie Weston
SECRET WEDDING	Emma Richmond
COLBY'S WIFE	Grace Green
STOLEN BRIDE	Sally Carr
FIRM COMMITMENT	Kate Denton

JoAnn ROSS

Southern Comforts

Welcome to Raintree, Georgia
—steamy capital of sin, scandal and murder

To her fans, Roxanne Scarborough is the queen of good taste. To her critics she is Queen Bitch. And now somebody wants her dead. When Chelsea Cassidy, Roxanne's official biographer, begins to unearth the truth about Roxanne's life, her investigation takes on a very personal nature—with potentially fatal consequences.

"JoAnn Ross delivers a sizzling, sensuous romance."

—Romantic Times

**AVAILABLE IN PAPERBACK
FROM MAY 1997**

FREE!

FOUR FREE
specially selected
Presents™ novels
PLUS a FREE Mystery Gift
when you return this page...

Return this coupon and we'll send you 4 Mills & Boon® Presents™ novels and a mystery gift absolutely FREE! We'll even pay the postage and packing for you.

We're making you this offer to introduce you to the benefits of the Reader Service™– FREE home delivery of brand-new Mills & Boon Presents novels, at least a month before they are available in the shops, FREE gifts and a monthly Newsletter packed with information, competitions, author profiles and lots more...

Accepting these FREE books and gift places you under no obligation to buy, you may cancel at any time, even after receiving just your free shipment. Simply complete the coupon below and send it to:

MILLS & BOON READER SERVICE, FREEPOST, CROYDON, SURREY, CR9 3WZ.

READERS IN EIRE PLEASE SEND COUPON TO PO BOX 4546, DUBLIN 24

NO STAMP NEEDED

Yes, please send me 4 free Presents novels and a mystery gift. I understand that unless you hear from me, I will receive 6 superb new titles every month for just £2.20* each, postage and packing free. I am under no obligation to purchase any books and I may cancel or suspend my subscription at any time, but the free books and gift will be mine to keep in any case. (I am over 18 years of age)

P7XE

Ms/Mrs/Miss/Mr_____
BLOCK CAPS PLEASE

Address_____

_____

_____ Postcode _____

Offer closes 30th November 1997. We reserve the right to refuse an application. *Prices and terms subject to change without notice. Offer only valid in UK and Ireland and is not available to current subscribers to this series. Overseas readers please write for details.

You may be mailed with offers from other reputable companies as a result of this application. Please tick box if you would prefer not to receive such offers. ☐

Mills & Boon® is a registered trademark of Harlequin Mills & Boon Limited.

New York Times bestselling author

Jayne Ann Krentz

Full Bloom

Part bodyguard, part troubleshooter, Jacob Stone
had, over the years, pulled Emily out of countless
acts of rebellion against her domineering family.
Now he'd been summoned to rescue her from a
disastrous marriage. Emily didn't want his
protection—she needed his love. But did Jacob
need this new kind of trouble?

"A master of the genre...nobody does it better!"

—Romantic Times

**AVAILABLE IN PAPERBACK
FROM MAY 1997**